**Her new boyfriend is rich, gentle, charming and *devilishly* handsome, but he may be too hot to handle. He's hiding a secret . . . and she's in for one Hell of a surprise.**

LUCY O'NEILL is a plain-Jane New York PR exec with a tiny apartment, a dead-end job, and a pair of annoyingly perfect roommates. Nothing exciting ever happens to her, until one night at a neighborhood pub . . .

Lewis Mephisto is tall, handsome, and hot. Very hot. He meets her gaze through the crowd, a wicked grin on his lips, an irresistible invitation in his eyes.

He's Mr. Right Times Ten. Sophisticated, wealthy, sexy, and completely devoted to her, body *and* soul. So what's her problem?

Can't she handle dating the Devil?

LEWIS LOOKS at me hard for a moment in the darkness, then nods. "So you've figured the whole thing out," he says ruefully.

"You're—"

"Yeah," he says.

"Say it," I say in a trembling voice. "I want you to say it."

He reaches over and switches his bedside lamp on, and suddenly the room is flooded with warm light. Then he looks back at me and shrugs. "I'm Satan," he says.

He looks so boyishly vulnerable, sitting there shirtless amidst the rumpled sheets, one sock on and one off, blinking sleep out of his blue eyes, that I want to laugh. Of course, I also want to cry. I can feel the tears welling up in the corners of my eyes, but I manage to keep my voice steady. "And you've been—all this time, you've been—trying to steal my soul?"

"Not *steal* it, exactly," he says. "Just . . . lead you into temptation."

# Dating the Devil

by

## Lia Romeo

Bell Bridge Books

This is a work of fiction. Names, characters, places and incidents are either the products of the author's imagination or are used fictitiously. Any resemblance to actual persons (living or dead), events or locations is entirely coincidental.

Bell Bridge Books
PO BOX 300921
Memphis, TN 38130
Print ISBN: 978-1-61194-252-1

Bell Bridge Books is an Imprint of BelleBooks, Inc.

We at BelleBooks enjoy hearing from readers.
Visit our websites – www.BelleBooks.com and www.BellBridgeBooks.com.

10 9 8 7 6 5 4 3 2 1

Cover design: Debra Dixon
Interior design: Hank Smith
Photo credits:
Pitchfork (manipulated) © Jiripravda | Dreamstime.com
Cocktail (manipulated) © Oblachko | Dreamstime.com

:Lddf:01:

# Dedication

To my friends, who've been there for me through all the adventures that inspired Lucy's adventures,

And to my family, who's been there for me through everything always,

And to Dan, love of my life

# – 1 –

MY FRIENDS and I play a game sometimes called "What's Your Personal Hell?"

If there were a Hell . . . and you were unfortunate enough to end up there . . . and the punishments were designed to be the worst possible thing for each particular person . . . what would yours be? What's the worst thing you could imagine suffering for all eternity?

For my friend Natalie, it would be a world without men.

Natalie likes meeting men almost as much as she likes crushing their dreams of settling down in a cute little house and making babies . . . dreams which she seems to inspire in every man she meets, though she has no intention of doing any such thing.

She's stunning—over six feet in her perpetual three-inch heels, with green eyes, black hair, and a wardrobe of minis and micro-minis and even-smaller-than-micro-minis by obscure Italian designers. Plus, she's what they call "independently wealthy" . . . meaning she doesn't really have to have a job. She does a bit of modeling, but mostly devotes herself to seducing the city's most eligible bachelors—and the city's least eligible bachelors—and pretty much all the bachelors in between. I'd definitely hate her if she weren't my best friend.

For my other best friend, Melissa, her personal Hell would be a messy apartment that never got clean.

Melissa was the valedictorian of our graduating class at Cornell, earned her MBA at Columbia, and now works as a management consultant. She puts in eighty hour weeks, and still manages to find time to keep the apartment we all share spotless (Natalie and I tend to throw our clothes on the floor and leave half-empty containers of Haagen-Dazs melting on the kitchen counters), train for the New York City Marathon—oh, and spend time with Brandon, whom she met in the MBA program. He's now a V.P. at a successful software company, and he recently put a sparkling three carat diamond on her perfectly manicured finger.

Mel's beautiful too—blonde and petite and impeccably put together, from her pencil skirts to her blazers to the string of pearls that never leaves her neck. Needless to say, when the three of us go out, I don't get a lot of attention.

Me? My personal Hell would be spending eternity dating in New York.

When I first moved to the city after college, I had things all figured out. I had the perfect job as an account executive at a boutique public relations firm, and the perfect adorable apartment in Chelsea with my perfect boyfriend, Ben.

Ben was tall, with blond curls and ruddy cheeks, and we'd been together since freshman year of college. We'd met on a volunteer trip over spring break, building houses for Habitat for Humanity down in Georgia. He looked good swinging a shovel, and even better over beers at the dive bar we used our fake IDs to sneak into that night. He was the first boy I ever loved, the first boy I ever slept with, the first . . . everything.

A year and a half after we moved to New York, he dumped me.

He was too young to be in such a committed relationship, he was trying to find himself, he was feeling like he needed to concentrate on his friends and his work. He was also, I found out later, sleeping with one of his coworkers at his hedge fund.

After the breakup, I couldn't afford our apartment on my own . . . and Ben could, so he stayed there. Me? I moved in with Mel and Nat. They were sharing a Murray Hill two bedroom which happened to have a giant walk-in closet in the front hallway . . . so out went Nat's designer outfits, and in went a full-size bed, an IKEA lamp . . . and me.

Two years later, I'm still here. My makeshift "room" lacks certain amenities, like, say, windows, or the ability to get out the door without climbing over the bed . . . but I'm only paying five hundred dollars a month, which allows me to afford cute clothes and bar tabs on a PR girl's salary. And thanks to Mel's cleaning habits and Nat's West Elm addiction, the rest of the apartment is beautiful, decorated with tasteful modern furniture in soft browns and tans. I spend a lot of time hanging out in the living room.

And I spend a lot of time out. Dating. Or at least I have been, though I'm pretty much ready to give up at this point.

After Ben and I broke up, Nat and Mel took me out to our local wine bar, treated me to bruschetta and a bottle of pinot grigio, and told me I needed to be single for a while. They said I needed to focus on my work, spend time with my friends, concentrate on my hobbies, and give myself time to heal. I told them they were totally right.

I signed up for Match.com the next day.

And eHarmony . . . and OkCupid . . . and J-Date, even though I'm not Jewish. I placed a personal ad on Craigslist, in which I described myself as "newly single and looking to have some fun," and received three hundred pictures of penises within the next twenty minutes. Apparently, "fun" on Craigslist is code for sex. I'd been thinking more in terms of afternoons at the museum and evenings at wine bars.

And I dated. I dated Chris from Craigslist—one of the few respondents who *hadn't* sent me a picture of his penis. I found out three dates later that this was probably because he didn't have one . . . Chris, née Christine, was a pre-op transsexual. I wanted to be open-minded, but I had to confess that a penis was on my list of non-negotiable requirements.

I dated Sam from Match. Sam asked me to dinner, then back to his Park Avenue apartment . . . which, it turned out, was actually his parents' Park Avenue apartment. In which he liked to have threesomes. Which included his dad.

I dated Stu from eHarmony, who (despite the fact that his name was Stu) I actually thought had potential. We went for coffee and had such a nice time that we decided to go for dinner, at which we had such a nice time that we decided to go for after-dinner drinks. He kissed me goodnight and texted me the next day to ask me to come over and watch a movie. So I did . . . and it was porn. Gay porn. And after insisting for a while that gay porn just helped to get him in the mood, Stu finally allowed me to stammer my excuses and make my escape.

And I dated Josh and Alex and Mike and Roger and John 1 and John 2 and Evan and Geoffrey and Steve and Ryan and Greg. Some of them I met online, some I met out at bars, some in bookstores or coffee shops or even on the subway . . . but we never managed to make it beyond the third date. And now I'm finally thinking it's time to give up on the whole thing for a while.

Nat approves. She's never had any trouble meeting guys—it's more that she has trouble getting rid of them—so she doesn't understand why I'm trying so hard to find someone to date. She wants me to go out to the bars with her every weekend. Even though when I do, she always ends up making out with someone, and I end up sitting at the bar by myself or standing outside bumming cigarettes from the bouncer.

Ever since Mel got engaged, though, she's decided that everyone else should too . . . she's tried setting me up with three or four of Brandon's friends already. She tells me that I can find the perfect guy and be just as happy as she is, but I've started thinking maybe I don't believe her.

I've started thinking maybe it really *is* impossible to find the perfect guy in New York . . . at least for a girl from Kansas with brown hair and chubby cheeks and pants from Gap, not Gucci. I've started thinking it's time to stop trying for a while.

And of course . . . as soon as I decide to stop trying, I meet Lewis.

# – 2 –

IT'S A SATURDAY night in September. Mel's fiancé is out of town, and Nat's finally managed to ditch the latest guy who's been calling and texting and leaving flowers with our doorman. And because of my new plan—giving up on all the losers in New York and being a strong, single woman—I haven't scheduled any dates for this weekend, so we decide to have a girls' night.

Not only that, but we decide to have a girls' night at the first bar the three of us ever went to together. It's a dive in the Village called the Peculier Pub. When we were freshmen in college, Nat's cousin was a junior at NYU, so one fall weekend the three of us packed our duffel bags full of our skimpiest outfits and took the five-hour bus ride from Cornell down to the city.

Nat's cousin Jason, who Mel and I decided was secretly in love with her (but who wasn't?), told us he'd take us out that night, but first we had to get some fake IDs. They didn't have to be good, especially since we were girls . . . we just had to show the bouncers *something*. He took us to a souvenir shop in Times Square, where we ducked down a narrow flight of stairs into the basement, and had our pictures taken and plastered onto "state identification cards" that declared that we were twenty-two years old and from Ohio. Then we each put on about four pounds of makeup (I didn't usually wear any, but Mel and Nat convinced me that it would help me look older) and headed out to the bars.

Our first stop was a Union Square lounge called Lemon, where the bouncer took one look at my fake ID, made a shooing motion and shook his head. Then Jason took us to Peculier Pub.

It was a dark, wooden dive packed with bodies and pulsing music. In high school, I'd been first chair violinist of the local youth symphony and spent all my spare time practicing, so I'd hardly even gone to any parties. Now my violin was tucked away neatly on a shelf in my parents' house in Kansas, and I was determined to turn myself into a worldly college vixen. The faint smell of vomit wafting from the open doorway suggested that this would be a perfect place to start.

We made sure Nat stood in line first this time. She was wearing a deep red V-neck shirt that showed off cleavage that could easily belong to a twenty-two-year-old. The bouncer hardly even glanced at her ID, he was so busy staring at her breasts, and once he let her in he waved the rest of us in after her.

It was Fleet Week, and sailors started buying us shots, and pretty soon Mel and I were dancing on top of one of the wooden tables while Nat was wearing one of the sailors' hats and making out with another one in the corner, Jason watching her with a look of equal parts irritation and longing.

That night I smoked my first cigarette and kissed my first stranger. I'd kissed my high school boyfriend, a sweet Chinese boy named Charlie Yang who was a flutist. We'd even indulged in some cautious groping over the summer, reaching furtively up each other's shirts in the back seat of his parents' Volvo, parked on dark streets far away from both his house and mine.

He was going to the University of Kansas, and when I left for Cornell, we'd promised to stay together, but after a month he'd sent me an email saying he was dating Anna Barnett, the pianist who'd beaten me out to win the Lawrence Concerto Competition by one vote the previous year. My resulting despair was part of the motivation for our New York weekend.

But now Mel and I were up on the table, shaking our hips to AC/DC, and there were boys all around us, and one of them was grabbing my hand and pushing his hips against mine. He leaned in close and shouted in my ear that his name was Philip, and I shouted that mine was Lucy, and then he was shaking a pack of cigarettes in my face, saying "Do you smoke?"

I didn't, of course, but I said I did, and then we were outside, and instead of giving me a cigarette he was leaning towards me and putting his tongue in my mouth. We kissed for a while, there on the sidewalk, and then we shared a cigarette, me taking tiny puffs so I wouldn't cough, and then we kissed some more and he put his hands on my waist under my black silk halter (borrowed from Nat) and told me I was beautiful. And then it was four a.m. and Mel and Nat and I were walking down the street arm in arm, singing "Oh What a Night" at the top of our lungs, and Jason was trailing behind us, looking like he wished he could put us back on the bus to Cornell right that minute.

I don't think we'd been back to the Peculier Pub since then. The next time we were all in the city together was after we were legal, so we could pick places to go without worrying about how strict they were about fake IDs. And after college, when we moved to Manhattan, Mel decided she didn't go to dive bars anymore, so we usually ended up sipping saketinis or champagne cocktails at places with vaguely Asian names and leather banquettes.

But tonight we'd ordered Chinese food and a couple of bottles of wine to go with it (I've got my share of problems with living in New York, but being able to have a bottle of wine delivered to your door makes up for a lot), and ended up mostly ignoring the Moo Shu in favor of the pinot. So by ten p.m., when Nat said, "You know what'd be fun?" even Mel was tipsy enough to agree with her.

Now our cab is making its slow way through the giggling hordes of drunken NYU students on Bleecker Street, and I'm starting to have second thoughts. I'll be twenty-seven in a couple of months, and most of these girls look like they haven't even cracked the big two-oh yet. They have blonde streaks in their hair and glitter on their eyelids and it's clear that no one has ever broken their hearts.

But I'm wearing a short black Marc Jacobs dress which had been Mel's until she got tired of it, and which has the remarkable effect of pushing my stomach in while pushing my breasts out, and a necklace of bright coral beads I bought from a street vendor. I've blow dried my shoulder length brown hair straight, even bothered to use Mel's flatiron to smooth the ends of it, and Nat's lent me her coral lipstick, which matches my necklace. I don't normally wear lipstick, but I have to admit I like the way it turns my mouth from a very ordinary thing, a thing to use for chewing a pen or taking a bite of a sandwich, into a vivid slash of color meant for kissing or pursing seductively around a cigarette. I look good.

Of course, not compared to my friends I don't. Mel wears a short, charcoal grey pencil skirt and a ruffled ivory blouse, her shoulder-length blonde hair straight and shiny, her signature strand of pearls around her neck, and a tiny Louis Vuitton bag that would cost me a month's salary casually slung over her shoulder. As usual, she's spent an hour on her makeup, and as usual it's perfect . . . creamy skin, smoky eyes, flawless red lips. Minutes before we left, Nat shimmied into a deep green mini-dress, dabbed on some sparkly silver shadow and fuchsia lipstick, and tossed her keys and her credit card into a black fringed leather clutch, and despite the fact that she's hardly spent any time she still looks better than either of us.

The bouncer gives us a puzzled look when we come in the door. The three of us, in our designer dresses (hand-me-down, in my case, but still), are a far cry from the jeans and t-shirts crowd packed three deep waiting for beers at the bar. We've barely set foot in the place and we're already getting appreciative glances from guys, at least Mel and Nat are, and pretty soon we're sharing a booth with a group of investment bankers and they've put a round of shots on the table in front of us.

An hour and several rounds later, Natalie and one of the bankers are whispering seductively in each other's ears on the other side of the table, and Mel and another one have disappeared into the alcove beside the bathroom. Something I forgot to mention about Mel is that, despite having a perfect fiancé, she cheats on him from time to time.

It's never anything serious. She'll get a little too close to a guy at a bar while they're dancing, and they'll kiss. Or she'll come back from a party that Brandon couldn't go to with a story about making out with somebody in the bathroom. She's never actually gone home with anyone, or if she has, she's been back in her bed by early the next morning. And she always feels bad afterwards, though never bad enough not to do it again.

I don't actually *know* that she's kissing the banker—who's very cute, six feet tall with short brown hair and a blue button-down shirt that matches his eyes—in the tiny alcove next to the bathroom that used to hold a telephone. I don't really want to know, which is why even though I've had to pee for the last twenty minutes I've been holding it.

I don't like Brandon that much—he was born and raised in New York, went to NYU and Columbia, and definitely sees the rest of the country as flyover territory. And he has a habit of looking at my handbag (usually cheap) and my shoes (usually cheaper), as though he's measuring my worth by what I'm wearing. Until I met him, I thought only salespeople in snooty boutiques did that.

But despite being kind of a snob, he doesn't deserve what Mel's doing—and if I see it, I'm going to feel like I have to pull her aside and tell her so. We've had these conversations before, and they always end with her crying and telling me I'm right, and then the next time she gets drunk going out and doing it again.

I'm making half-hearted conversation with the banker on my side of the table. He's clearly The Friend That's Not Cute—he's short and bald and wears wire-rimmed glasses. Which would be fine, if he had anything interesting to say, but he's talking about derivatives . . . and even if I knew what derivatives were, I doubt I'd find them all that entertaining.

Also, he's got his arm around my shoulder, and his fingers are inching down towards my breast. So before he can actually grope me I jump up and with my brightest smile I tell him I'm going to the bathroom. If I see Mel, I'll just have to ignore her, that's all.

But I don't see Mel. In fact, I forget all about Mel, because I see Lewis.

Of course, I don't know he's Lewis yet. But I know he's got to be *someone*. He's standing against the wall, next to the jukebox. He's mostly in shadow, but the red and blue flashing lights from the jukebox are playing across his face. He's tall and dark-haired, and he's wearing a suit . . . a navy jacket and pants, and a white shirt, untucked, with the top two buttons undone so I get just a glimpse of his smooth, muscled chest.

But the thing I really notice is how *still* he is. Everyone else in the bar is in constant motion, sipping drinks, twirling hair, rocking back and forth to the beat. But he's standing perfectly motionless. There's a cocktail glass in his hand but he isn't drinking. Just standing . . . and looking.

Looking at me.

Really? I look over my shoulder. Maybe he's looking at Natalie. She's straddling the banker in the booth and they're kissing . . . definitely a spectacle worth looking at, but I don't think he could see them from where he's standing. I look behind me, to see if he's checking out one of the blonde coeds. But when I look back, he raises one eyebrow, and he smiles.

It isn't a very *nice* smile. It isn't the kind of smile that says, I'd like to get to know you, take you out to dinner, come home and make out on the couch, and then give you money for a taxi. It's the kind of smile that says, I'm going to eat you. And you're going to like it.

I don't usually go for the dangerous type. Nat goes crazy for them, and I know if she spots this guy it'll be goodbye banker, hello bad boy. And of course, if he spots her, he'll stop looking at me this way, and I suddenly, desperately don't want that to happen. Those shadowed eyes . . . that predatory smile. *But Grandmother, what big teeth you have!* The line from "Little Red Riding Hood" comes suddenly and inanely into my head.

He extends one finger and beckons. Who, me? I must have mouthed the question, because he nods and beckons again. I walk a few steps slowly towards him, my heels sticking to the wooden floor.

"You look like a lady who needs a drink," he says in a low, sexy voice.

I'm pretty sure that's the last thing I look like, seeing as I've had three? four? of the disgusting shots that the bankers were calling SoCo and vodka. ("Isn't SoCo supposed to go with lime?—not . . . vodka?" I'd asked The Friend That's Not Cute. He'd just shrugged.) I'm pretty sure my cheeks are flushed and my hair is sticking to my face, and I might just be wobbling a little. But his lips are so sexy, forming the shapes of the words, that all I can do is nod.

And suddenly, there are two drinks in his hands. I could have sworn there was only one before. He extends one of them towards me and the ice tinkles invitingly. I take a sip of the dark brown liquid, and despite the fact that I'm already tipsy I already am it burns all the way down.

"What *is* that?" I gasp when I can speak again.

"Scotch," he says, as though drinking scotch at a dive bar were the most natural thing in the world. "Very good scotch," he adds.

I try another small sip, and it goes down smoother this time. "Thank you," I manage.

"I take it you're not a scotch drinker."

"I usually drink wine."

"What kind?" he asks.

"White. Sauvignon blanc or pinot."

"Ah." He sips at his scotch, nodding as though he's got me all figured out.

"What do you mean, ah?"

"I have a theory," he says. "I spend a lot of time in bars. And I believe you can tell a lot about a person based on their libation of choice."

Libation? Who says *libation*? "So what can you tell about me?"

"White wine drinkers are usually cautious. They don't have adventurous tastes, but they want to seem worldly. They like wearing black. They go to the museum and the theater and the symphony a few times a year, but more because they feel like they're supposed to than because they really enjoy it."

"Hmm." He's mostly right. Despite the hundreds of good restaurants in our neighborhood, I tend to go the same few places all the time. I wear black every time I go out, mostly because it's slimming. And I would love to seem worldly, though I've pretty much realized it's a lost cause. I do genuinely love the New York Philharmonic, though. I go whenever I can afford a ticket—mostly by myself, though Nat's been known to go as an excuse to wear her dramatic black silk opera gloves. I've tried to tell her that they're supposed to be for the opera, not the symphony, but she doesn't care.

"So what about scotch drinkers?" I ask him.

"Complicated. Masochistic. Intelligent. Loyal."

"That kind of sounds like a sheepdog."

He laughs, throwing his head back, showing his white teeth, and his brooding, serious face is totally transformed. Making him laugh feels like the greatest accomplishment of my night—of my week, actually.

"I like you," he says.

"Even though I don't have adventurous tastes?"

"I think you might have more adventurous tastes than you realize. Maybe you just haven't found the perfect drink yet."

I take a big gulp of scotch to avoid meeting his eyes, then cough and sputter as it burns my throat. "Nope. Still terrible," I manage to choke out.

He smiles and takes a pack of cigarettes out of his suit pocket. "Smoke?"

I nod—I never smoke in the daytime, but I do occasionally when I go out—and he sets our glasses down on top of the jukebox, then takes my hand, pulling me through the crowd towards the front door. His hand is hot, and all of the nerves in my body seem to be concentrated in my fingers where they're touching his.

Outside, he takes a cigarette out of the pack, and leans forward to place it between my lips. "Want to see a party trick?" he says. He touches the tip of the cigarette with his index finger, and it flares into light.

"How did you . . .?"

He just smiles and lights his own cigarette the same way. We smoke for a moment in silence, watching women in bright cocktail dresses and men in dark suits, women with purple hair and men in leather pants go in and out of bars, climb in and out of cabs, disappear into the subway.

"You know what I love about New York?" he says.

"What?"

"How everyone's lost, but they all look like they know exactly where they're going."

"Do I look like I know where I'm going?" I ask him.

"No," he says. "But I bet you haven't been here very long. Have you?"

"Four years," I say. "How long have you been here?"

He smiles. "Forever."


ANOTHER CIGARETTE later, he's kissing my neck in the back seat of a cab headed downtown to his apartment.

Now I should say, first of all, that I'm not the kind of girl who normally lets strange men kiss my neck in the back seat of cabs. I'm not even the kind of girl who normally lets strange men take me home.

I had a couple of one night stands shortly after Ben and I broke up, woke up hung over and feeling bad about myself, and spent the next week hoping they'd call to make me feel better. They didn't. After that I decided sleeping with strangers just wasn't "me," and I'd only sleep with men I'd been dating for a while. Meaning I haven't had sex with anyone in almost two years.

But he kissed me outside the bar, while I was waiting for a taxi, and my knees literally buckled. I'd never experienced a truly remarkable kiss before. I'd enjoyed kissing, but more as proof that someone wanted to kiss me than as a sexual act.

But this.

It wasn't a kiss, it was a revelation. I was standing on the curb, about to stick my arm out, and he tipped my chin back with one finger, then leaned in and lightly brushed his lips against mine. My lips tingled. Then he leaned closer, gently biting my lip with his teeth and letting his tongue brush against my tongue, and my tongue was alive, electric, twisting eagerly around his. And then my knees went weak, and I was leaning against him, into him, as our lips, tongues, teeth met, parted, met again, and when a taxi finally drew alongside us he pulled me into the back seat and told the driver to go to Broadway and Rector Street.

And now his lips are on my neck and tongues of flame are licking up towards my hairline, and I'm biting my lip to keep myself from gasping and running my hands over his thigh muscles under the (very good quality) wool of his suit. I don't want the cab ride to end, because I don't want him to stop kissing me like this, but I also want to feel his tongue against my stomach, my thighs, my . . .

Finally, we pull up in front of a huge, old-fashioned apartment building in the financial district, tumble out of the cab, and make our way up the steps. Before he opens the door, he grabs my hair and crushes me against him, kissing me hard for a moment, and then we separate and walk with perfect decorum through the lobby. At least, he does. He even manages to nod cordially at the doorman. As for me, my face is flushed, and I'm still breathing heavily.

He presses the up arrow for the elevator, and as soon as the doors open and close behind us he's pressing me against the wall, kissing my collarbone and running his hands over my breasts under the tight fabric of the dress I'm wearing. I know we're on camera, but I don't care, I'm pulling the neckline of my dress down lower to feel his rough, hot hands on my skin. And then he pulls away, says "Wait," and the two of us stare at each other, faces inches apart, breathing hard, as the elevator moves slowly upwards towards the thirteenth floor. His eyes are deep blue, almost black. A single drop of sweat rolls down his forehead.

When the elevator doors open he fumbles in his pocket for keys, gets his door open and then pushes me up against the back of it. He hasn't bothered to turn on the lights, and the whites of his eyes gleam in the darkness. With one hand he's holding my shoulders against the door, while with the other he's pulling up my dress and pulling down my thong, and I'm fumbling frantically at his belt buckle. Finally, he lets me go for a minute and undoes it himself, letting his pants drop and pool around his ankles.

Then he quickly unwraps and unrolls a condom and pushes into me, and the heat spreads upwards through my entire body as he starts to move. My hands are clutching his shoulders, and I'm biting my lip to keep from screaming as the heat builds and builds until I feel as if I am literally combusting from the inside. And then I am screaming, and then we're finished and my knees are buckling and I'm sagging to the ground, still leaning against the door, and he's picking me up and carrying me into the bedroom, where we do it all again—twice, as a matter of fact—before finally falling into an exhausted sleep at five in the morning.

And there's one thing that's odd—very odd, actually, though I'm too drunk and dazed with lust to pay a lot of attention. The entire time, he refuses to take off his socks.

# – 3 –

I'M AWOKEN at nine a.m. by my cell phone ringing. Over and over again.

By the time I finally stagger out of bed, attempt to wrap a sheet around myself (how do women do this gracefully in movies?), give up wrestling with the sheet and walk across the room to retrieve my purse naked, I have seven missed calls. And they're all from my boss, Linda.

When I first moved to the city, my three-point-nine GPA and upbeat attitude quickly landed me a job as an account executive at a boutique PR firm. Shortly thereafter, I realized that "account executive" was code for "office bitch" and "boutique PR firm" was code for "only one client."

Said client is Kruger, a vacuum company, so I spend my days—and sometimes my nights, and often my weekends—writing press releases about the "incredible cleaning power" of the Kruger Turbo Mini Vac or trying to convince lifestyle editors to let me send them CDs with a demo of the "sleek and shiny" Kruger Sweeper. It's a tough job because, no matter how many creative adjectives we employ, there's really nothing sexy about vacuums. It's also a tough job because Linda is the most disorganized woman in the world.

I get back in bed, wrap the sheet around me, and check my voicemail. She's left three frantic messages, saying that she needs to get into the office right away to pick up one of the new Kruger StickVacs, not even available in stores, for a producer friend who wants to feature it in a segment on "Good Morning America." But she can't find her office keys, so she needs me to come over and let her in.

"Good Morning America" is big . . . but really? Sunday morning? And I know that once I get to the office, she'll ask if I can just take care of a few little things, and I won't get out of there until mid-afternoon. I think about pretending I lost my phone, going home and sleeping for a few more hours, then nursing my hangover with eggs and mimosas at a late brunch with Mel and Nat and telling them all about the crazy time I had last night.

Instead, I climb out of bed, retrieve my dress from the corner where he flung it last night, and pull it over my head. When I emerge from the black fabric, he's opened his eyes and is propped up on one elbow, watching me.

"I have to say, I liked it better when that dress was going the other direction," he says.

I blush. "I have to go in to work."

"I didn't think PR girls worked on Sundays."

Had I told him I worked in PR? "Most don't. My boss is . . ." I trail off. It would take too long to explain.

"What time do you get done?"

"Um. I don't know. Afternoon, probably."

"How about dinner?"

"Um. Really?" I'm stunned. I was definitely expecting this to be a onetime thing, though the sex was so amazing that I didn't care. And now, not only is he asking me out again, but he's asking me out before I've even left yet.

"Yes, really." He seems amused. "Eight p.m. There's a French place in the Village—A.O.C."

"Okay."

"Take my card. In case you get held up at work." He gets out of bed, naked except for his black socks, and retrieves a business card from the pocket of his suit jacket, tossed in the corner of the room. The card is printed in elegant calligraphy on thick, creamy paper.

*Lewis Mephisto*
*555-606-3516*
*Lewis.Mephisto@gmail.com*

I realize I hadn't even known his name. I turn the card over, looking for the name of a bank or a hedge fund—I figure he works in finance, since he lives in the financial district. But it doesn't say anything.

"So what do you do, Lewis?" I ask him.

He smiles. "I'm a recruiter."

I wait for more, but nothing else is forthcoming, and I have to get to the office. I put the business card into my purse and slip on my heels, wincing as they rub against blisters from last night. "Well. Um. I guess I'll see you tonight then."

"I'll see you tonight, Lucy."

Did I tell him my name last night? I must have. He probably told me his too and I just didn't remember.

On my way out, I notice what I was too, um, busy to pay attention to the night before: his apartment is gorgeous. It's huge—by New York standards, anyway, meaning the whole place is about the size of my parents' basement in Kansas—and looks like it's been professionally decorated. The walls are painted red and black and the furniture is teak and leather. There's a zebra print rug on the floor in the living room, and a painting in bold blocks of color that's probably an original something-or-other above the couch. It's very bachelor pad, but tasteful.

The whole place has an empty, un-lived-in feel, though. There aren't any magazines lying around half-read, or dirty dishes in the sink, or shoes kicked off next to the couch, or any of the other signs of human disorder that our apartment is full of despite Mel's best efforts. I somehow get the sense that he's not there all that often.

I take a cab uptown, stopping only to buy a cream-colored cardigan at the Gap to make my outfit from last night marginally more work-appropriate. I'd love to go home and shower, but I've gotten two more frantic calls from Linda and reassured her that I'll be there in fifteen minutes. There's nothing I can do about my hair, a snarl of tangles—I have a quick flashback of him pulling on it last night—so I pull it back as tightly as I can with the rubber band I have around my wrist.

In the cab, I send a quick text to Mel and Nat: "Omg—met

the hottest guy last night and SLEPT w him—and having dinner tonight! Can I borrow an outfit?" Then I pay the driver seventeen dollars (seventeen dollars! This is what I get for having sleepovers in the financial district) and get out, mentally readying myself for a long day.

Our office is in a grungy building in the garment district. To get in, you actually have to go through the store on the ground floor, which sells silk at wholesale prices, and then up a dimly lit staircase to the fifth floor.

When Kruger comes in to town for business meetings, Linda rents a conference room at the Marriott. But we do all our work here because of the incredibly low rent she gets from Abdul, the owner of the silk store—and of the building—who Linda is sleeping with. (Okay, that's just my theory. She calls him a "very dear friend," but I don't have any "very dear friends" who take me on Caribbean vacations, and Linda and Abdul spent last New Year's together in the Bahamas. But Linda went through a rough divorce a few years ago, and I think she deserves any "very dear friends" she can get.)

Linda is standing outside, wearing a cream-colored cashmere turtleneck . . . and her pajama bottoms. At least my outfit is more work-appropriate than *that*. She's wearing glasses and her hair is a rat's nest. "Lucy, thank God!" she exclaims as soon as she sees me, and begins talking a mile a minute about how incredible it would be if we could actually get the "Good Morning America" placement, and how urgent it is that she messenger the sample over to their offices immediately.

Upstairs, we whip up a quick press release for the StickVac, which is so new that we haven't even come up with any marketing materials yet. Then we take a few "beauty shots" of the vac against a black background, and one "action shot" of me, in my black dress and heels, vacuuming with it (okay, so maybe it's a good thing that I'm still wearing this outfit!)

A few hours later, we've put together a credible press kit, which we messenger over to Linda's producer friend along with the sample. And when her friend calls to tell her she's planning to feature the StickVac on Friday's segment, Linda gives me a huge hug and tells me she couldn't have done it without me, which almost makes up for the nine a.m. phone call (almost).

It's two p.m. at this point—plenty of time to go home and nap before dinner (okay, and stop at Aldo to buy a pair of leopard print pumps, which will be perfect with the sexy black silk top I'm hoping Nat's going to let me borrow). Except that when I walk into the apartment, Nat is having a séance in the living room.

Nat's father died when she was twelve, leaving her with a lot of money (which is why she can afford to live in New York without really working, aside from the occasional modeling job) and a strong belief in the supernatural. Every few weeks, she tries to contact her dad in the great beyond, which involves pulling the shades, lighting candles and incense, and playing AC/DC—his favorite band—at maximum volume. She says sometimes she feels his presence, though she hasn't yet succeeded in having an actual conversation . . . though, what with the AC/DC, I'm not sure how she would.

So after trying to nap for an hour or so, I give up, take a shower, and (once the séance is over) drag Nat to Starbucks for lattes and gossip. Mel is spending the day hiking in the Catskills with Brandon. But Nat is excited enough for both of them, squealing over all the details of my wild night and telling me all about her own, which featured unsatisfying sex with the banker, and then much more satisfying sex with a guy she used to date, who sent her a late-night text shortly after she'd kicked the banker out of bed. So now the guy she used to date is obsessed with her again—he's texted her fourteen times today already—and it's going to be *so annoying* to convince him all over again that she's not actually interested (despite the satisfying sex). I try to look appropriately sympathetic.

Back at the apartment, Nat helps me get ready for dinner—her black silk top, my own dark denim jeans, the leopard print heels, and smoky eye makeup, which, despite having taken the same tutorial at Saks that Nat and Mel did, I can never manage to do on myself without looking like a Gothic clown.

I take the subway downtown, having spent enough on cab fare today already. I'm half-expecting him to stand me up, but he's waiting outside on the sidewalk, smoking a cigarette and looking unbelievably handsome in jeans and a navy blazer over a pale blue button-down. I start to blush just looking at him.

The restaurant is small and romantic, dark wood on the walls and candles on the tables. We're escorted to a tiny table near the window. Lewis takes a quick glance at the wine list, then orders a bottle of '84 viognier.

"If you like pinot, I think you'll like this," he says. "I'm trying to expand your horizons, but gently." He says it with such a sexy sardonic smile that I can't be irritated.

While we're sipping the wine—which is excellent—he asks me about work. To my relief, he's easy to talk to. (I wasn't sure, given that the night before we hadn't, um, done much talking.) He asks all the right questions in all the right places, and over grapes and brie, and then a delicious roasted chicken dish that we share, I find myself telling him all about it: my tiny, cluttered office, my low salary, my frustrations with spending my days describing vacuums. A few times I try to ask him questions about what he does, but he always turns the conversation deftly back in my direction—which is honestly such a nice change from most of the men I date that I let him.

And then he says: "I could get you a new job."

"What?" I sputter, spraying tiny drops of viognier onto the table. He's enough of a gentleman not to notice.

"I know some people at some of the bigger firms. Edelman, maybe, or Cohn & Wolfe. I'd just have to trade in a couple of favors."

"Seriously?"

I'm not sure why I believe that he could actually get me a job, especially with the economy the way it is. Maybe it's the confidence with which he says it. Maybe it's his apartment, which has to be upwards of five thousand dollars a month—anyone with that much money has got to have some connections. Or maybe it's just that he's so incredibly sexy that I can't imagine anyone denying him anything.

I have a vision of myself, dressed in a slimming black suit and sky high heels . . . never mind that I can't walk in anything much higher than a couple of inches. I'm striding along the sidewalk, heads turning admiringly as I walk by, towards a set of double glass doors. I toss my hair, pull open the doors and enter the sun-filled lobby, then ascend the staircase to my office (without tripping on my sky high heels, of course) and begin making phone calls to important media people.

"Besides," he says, "Kruger's a pretty big client. And you've had a lot of contact with them, right?"

"Sure, yeah. I talk to their CEO all the time." I'm always calling Jeff Boseman to go over product details, and we have strategy meetings with him at least once a month.

"So if you were to jump ship . . . you might be able to bring the client with you?"

"Oh. I don't know. Would that be . . .?"

"Necessary?" he says. "Probably. With the economy the way it is, nobody's hiring anyone who can't prove they can bring in business . . ."

The vision in my head changes, and now I'm picturing Linda. She's sitting on the floor of our tiny office, surrounded by piles of clutter—which she undoubtedly would be without me to organize everything for her. She's wearing her pajamas and tearing at her hair . . . because the business she's spent the past four years building . . . that she and I have spent the past four years building . . . is gone.

"I can't," I say. He gives me an incredulous look. I *did* just spend the past half hour complaining about my job. "I can't do that to Linda."

"You don't owe your boss anything," he says.

"I do, though. She gave me a job when I first moved to the city and nobody else would. I can't just up and steal her only client."

"It wouldn't be stealing. If the client chose to come with you, it would be because they felt you were the best woman for the job."

"Yeah, I—I know, but I can't. I really can't." He looks

down. Somehow I feel like I've disappointed him. "It's not that I don't appreciate your offer—I do, I really do, I just—Linda and I have worked together for a long time, and I just wouldn't feel right about it."

He raises his eyebrows and shrugs. "Dessert?"

Half an hour and half of a decadent chocolate mousse later, I find myself in a cab headed back to his apartment. I'd planned to give him a goodnight kiss, go home, and finally get some sleep, but the goodnight kiss had been so electrifying that when he'd hailed a taxi and asked me, "One stop?" I hadn't even wanted to stop kissing long enough to say yes.

So now we're wrapped around each other in the back seat of the cab, and being at least somewhat sober this time, I'm embarrassed about it . . . not embarrassed enough to stop, of course, but enough to be relieved when we've made it out of the cab and into the privacy of his apartment. We're lying on his king-sized bed and I'm down to my red lace bra and thong (my best set), and he's kissing my collarbone, leaving tiny, fiery imprints on my skin, and I'm fumbling with his belt buckle, though I'm too distracted by his lips to be able to actually unfasten it. And that's when I smell something burning. And I don't mean figuratively. Sure, my skin feels like it's on fire . . . but something is actually burning, too, and it's somewhere nearby.

When I was young, about five years old, I was in the kitchen with my mom while she was cooking dinner. I wanted to help, so I stood on tiptoes to stir the boiling pot of spaghetti, and my long, straggly brown hair got too close to the gas burner and caught flame. I started screaming, and my mom grabbed a rolled-up newspaper and frantically beat the flames out. I escaped with nothing more serious than hair that was long on one side and singed shoulder length on the other, and an exciting story to tell my friends the next day at school. But what I'd never forgotten was the harsh, sulfurous odor . . . the same odor I'm smelling now.

"Stop," I say, sitting up and pulling away from him.

"What?" He tries to pull me back down and start kissing me

again.

"Do you smell that?"

"What? No. I don't smell anything."

This isn't exactly surprising. I have an unusually sensitive sense of smell. I can't even wear perfume because it smells so overpoweringly, cloyingly sweet to me. "Something's burning," I say.

"No it isn't," he says, and bends down to graze my breasts with his lips.

"No, seriously." The burning smell has gotten stronger, and it seems to be coming from the front hallway. I get out of bed, wearing only my red bra and thong.

"Lucy, wait," he says. "Everything's fine. Come back to bed."

I ignore him and follow my nose down the hallway. The odor's getting stronger. It seems to be coming from the front hall closet. But how would something have caught on fire in the closet? I don't see any smoke coming out from under the door.

Well, maybe it is just in my head. I open the closet door . . . and scream.

The inside of the closet is a raging inferno of flames, from floor to ceiling, leaping and twisting and hitting me in the face with a blast of heat. I slam the door shut again. He's in the hallway now, and I grab his hand, pulling him out the door. "Fire! Fire! Your apartment's on fire! We have to go! We have to run! Come on! Quick!"

# — 4 —

FIFTEEN MINUTES later, Lewis and I, along with hundreds of other people, are huddled on the sidewalk outside his building. I'm shivering from a combination of shock and cold, wearing nothing but my underwear and a blanket that Lewis had the presence of mind to grab on our way out. I've wrapped it around me sarong-style, but it doesn't come down very far, and there's a lot of bare thigh visible.

I would be embarrassed, except that the woman next to me is in a camisole and a thong. She's explaining to the crowd of men who've gathered around her that she sleeps this way, and she was so disoriented when the fire alarm woke her up that she didn't think to put any pants on. Though somehow she did have the presence of mind to slip on a pair of feathered mules. She's tall and blonde, and I can't help sneaking envious glances at her perfectly toned, tanned ass, so different from my white, dimply one.

Lewis, however, hasn't even glanced in her direction. He's wrapped me solicitously in the crook of his arm, and he's telling me not to worry, everything's going to be fine. His fingers are five individual prints of heat on my bare skin. I have the sense that I should be reassuring *him*, given that it's his apartment that's on fire, but he doesn't seem particularly worried.

In fact, he seems as completely at ease here, standing on the street in his socks and jeans and half-unbuttoned shirt, as he did in the bar last night or the restaurant earlier this evening. I wonder if he ever went through an awkward phase, if there's a pimply-faced Lewis with braces and a bad haircut hidden in photo albums somewhere in his mother's basement, or if he's always been this effortless, this comfortable in his own smooth, tanned skin.

After a few minutes, the firefighters come downstairs, sweaty and streaked with ash, and tell us they've put the fire out and everybody can go back inside. Lewis squeezes my shoulder. "See?" he says. "I told you everything would be fine."

Everybody except Lewis and me, that is—says the tall, dark-haired fireman, older than the others, who has the words "Deputy Chief" on his helmet. He has to ask us a couple of questions. Lewis asks him if we can talk inside, and I hurry gratefully into the warmth of the lobby. Late September nights in New York are unpredictable, sometimes balmy and sometimes cold. This is one of the cold ones—it couldn't be much more than sixty degrees. A pleasant temperature in a long-sleeved shirt and jeans, but not such a pleasant temperature in a thong and a blanket.

Inside, I clutch my blanket tightly around me, trying to shield my mostly bare body from the stares of five uniformed firefighters. Although they are kind of cute . . . young, clean-cut, well-muscled, eyes bright in faces streaked dark with soot. But none as good-looking as Lewis, I decide with satisfaction. I used to play this game when I was with Ben—every time I saw an attractive man on the street, I'd ask myself: "Is he as cute as my boyfriend?" With Ben, I often had to admit that the answer was yes. Ben was boyishly handsome, and he looked nice in a suit, but he was basically ordinary. But in the last twenty-four hours, I haven't seen a single man I find as attractive as Lewis. Not that Lewis is my boyfriend, of course.

"Damnedest thing I've ever seen," the assistant fire chief is saying. "A fireproof closet."

A fireproof closet? Why would anyone want a fireproof *closet*?

"What made you think to do that?" the fireman continues.

"I didn't," Lewis says. "It must have been the previous owners."

"You didn't put in the sheet metal? Or the flame-retardant rubber around the door?"

"No," Lewis says. "I had no idea. I don't even use that closet—I've got plenty of storage space in the bedroom."

"Do you have any idea how the fire started?" I ask the fireman.

"Well, that's the strangest thing about it. Like you said, Mr. . . ."

"Mephisto."

"Right—there was nothing in there. If there had been, we would've seen ashes. So how does a fire start in a fireproof closet with nothing in it to burn?"

He looks at us as if he expects us to answer his question.

"I don't know," Lewis says. Suddenly there's a dangerous edge to his voice. "But I hope you're not suggesting I had something to do with it. Because I have an excellent alibi." He looks at me and smiles sideways, and I blush bright red.

"No," the fireman says, "There's no evidence of any accelerant—no traces of gasoline, turpentine, anything like that. So unless you started the fire out of thin air, then no, I don't think you had anything to do with it." He frowns, shaking his head. "It's damned strange, though. I've heard of these spontaneous combustion events . . . but I never thought I'd actually see one. You folks were lucky, that's all I can say," he says.

I nod fervently, shivering as I think about what might have happened. Even though it's almost two a.m. and I'm standing in Lewis' lobby wearing a blanket, I'm feeling like a very lucky girl right about now.

And I'm feeling even luckier when we're back upstairs ten minutes later, inspecting the closet. The flame-retardant rubber, which runs all the way around the door, has melted slightly—which is what I'd smelled burning. The edge of the rug where it meets the sheet metal floor of the closet is charred. There's a lingering chemical smell from whatever the firemen sprayed in there, and smudges of dirt from their boots on the hallway carpet. The sheet metal walls of the closet are still glowing faintly red, and Lewis warns me not to touch them. But other than that, it's like the fire never happened.

"A fireproof closet. Why would anyone do that?" I wonder aloud.

"I don't know," Lewis says. "Maybe it's some kind of anti-terrorism thing." His building is in what would have been the shadow of the World Trade Center, so that actually makes sense. "In any case, it isn't the strangest thing I've seen in New York. I knew a woman who turned her spare bedroom into a stable for her horse."

"What?" I start laughing. "That poor horse!"

"She lived uptown," Lewis says, "near the park, so she'd take the horse out late at night in the service elevator and ride it around the reservoir. She actually got away with it for almost a year, until one of the doormen caught her and called animal welfare."

"That's terrible."

"I know," he says. "And speaking of terrible . . ." He steps closer, unwrapping the blanket and revealing the scraps of red lace that are all I'm wearing underneath. "We were interrupted at a very inopportune moment before."

He leans in to kiss me and my knees go weak—literally weak—again. How does he do this to me? He takes my hand and pulls me back into the bedroom, pushing me down on the bed.

"Wait," I say. "That's not fair. I'm already practically naked—you have to take your clothes off too."

Slowly, he begins unbuttoning his shirt. I want to grab him, pull him in and taste his skin with my tongue, but I make myself wait until he takes his pants off and lies down beside me. He's wearing nothing but a pair of boxer briefs . . . and his socks.

The socks again. I want to ask him about it . . . but I'm afraid he might have some sort of foot fungus and it would be embarrassing and completely ruin the moment. And besides, he's kissing me again, and our bodies are melting together, his lips trailing over my neck, my breasts, my stomach, and then he's driving me absolutely insane with his tongue while I'm clutching the bed sheets, trying not to scream, and then he's unrolling a condom so we can finish what we started, and he could be wearing a pair of pink fuzzy unicorn slippers on his feet for all I care.

It turns out that almost dying in a fiery blaze is an excellent aphrodisiac. We don't actually end up getting to sleep until four.

I STUMBLE INTO work bleary-eyed the next morning, having gotten about six hours of sleep in the past two days. My hair is wet and I'm not wearing any makeup, since I opted for hitting the snooze button on the alarm Lewis thoughtfully set for me instead of getting up in time to put it on. I made a quick stop at my apartment to shower and change, then walked the six blocks over to the office, picking up an extra-large coffee from a street vendor on the way.

I flick on the office lights—Linda's not in yet—and then gasp in surprise. Sitting on my desk is an enormous bouquet of flowers—yellow sunflowers, purple larkspur, red and orange daisies, bursting out of a crystal vase tied with a red satin ribbon. A small white card sits on top.

> *Thanks for a lovely night. Hope to see you again soon.*
> *—Lewis*

I start up my computer, take his card out of my wallet and open my email.

*To: Lewis.Mephisto@gmail.com*
*From: ILoveLucy32345@yahoo.com*
*9:36 am*
*Re: Flowers*
*Thank you thank you THANK YOU!!!*

*To: ILoveLucy32345@yahoo.com*
*From: Lewis.Mephisto@gmail.com*
*9:45 am*
*RE:re:Flowers*
*Figured I owed you something, since I kept you up so late last night ;) Speaking of which, when can we do that again?*

*To: Lewis.Mephisto@gmail.com*
*From: ILoveLucy32345@yahoo.com*

*9:53 am*
*RE:re:re:Flowers*
*Um, I don't know . . . on my lunch break?*

I have to say—again—that I'm really not this kind of girl. Natalie's always running off to meet some lawyer or doctor or banker for a lunchtime quickie, and even Melissa and Brandon have been known to lock her office door and spend a few minutes on top of her desk. But not me. Even when I was having regular sex—back when I was with Ben—it was usually at night, and always in our bed. Not in the tiny bathroom in the hallway outside the office, which is where I find myself come one-thirty, with my legs wrapped around Lewis and my mouth smashed against his shoulder so Linda won't hear us.

Afterwards, we walk down the street to my favorite falafel place and order pitas stuffed with falafel and hummus and lettuce and tomato and yogurt sauce. Lewis pays, which is sweet, because it's not as though this is a proper date or anything. We sit at the counter to eat, and end up chatting about books—we're both big Stephen King fans, though Lewis thinks *Misery* is his best and I'm a fan of *The Stand*. The sun shines through the window, and everything seems to sparkle—the glass, the counter, the rows of sodas in the refrigerator case. I haven't felt this happy in a long time.

After we're done eating, he walks me back to the office. It's almost three p.m., and I ask him if he isn't supposed to be back at work.

"No," he says. "I make my own hours. I'm sort of an independent contractor."

It's the most he's told me about his job, and I press him for more. "So what does that mean? You do recruiting for a bunch of different companies?"

"Mostly just one," he says. "But I'm not on staff. I'm more of a freelance headhunter."

"So what's the company?"

We're in front of my building, and Lewis leans down and gives me a kiss. It lasts for a long time, and I'm just about ready to pull him upstairs and into the bathroom again, but I've already taken an hour-and-a-half lunch break. Reluctantly, I break away.

"I'll see you soon," he says, touching me on the tip of the nose with one finger. As always, his touch leaves an impression of heat behind on my skin. Then he heads off down the sidewalk.

It isn't until I'm halfway up the stairs that I realize he never answered my question.

# – 5 –

THE NEXT TWO weeks are perfect. Literally perfect. I spend almost every night with Lewis, except for Friday, when Mel and Nat drag me out to Vinoteca, the wine bar around the corner, because they haven't seen me all week. And then, between mouthfuls of tuna carpaccio and sips of sauvignon blanc, I spend the whole night *talking* about Lewis, causing Nat to roll her eyes and Mel to clap her hands delightedly. I still can't figure out what he sees in *me*, but when I share this concern with my friends they tell me I'm an idiot—and also that I'm amazing, despite being an idiot, and any guy, including Lewis, would be lucky to have me.

And he *does* seem to think he's lucky to have me, baffling as that may be. He emails during work, calls after, sets up plans to meet at one or another cozy, charming restaurant. He pulls out my chair, asks me questions about my day, pays for dinner and the cab ride back to his place which inevitably follows.

And in bed, he's more attentive than anyone I've ever met . . . he seems to know exactly which touch will make me shiver, which will make me scream, and when to use them, and it's like nothing I've ever experienced before. And to be fair, he seems to be enjoying himself just as much, though I'm not sure how that's possible.

He still keeps his socks on. Every time. And I still want to ask him about it, but I can't think of a way to do it without sounding awkward. Besides, I'm usually very quickly . . . distracted.

Sometimes after we have sex we fall asleep right away. Other times he lights a cigarette—with his fingertip, a trick I still can't figure out. I've asked him to show me how it works, but he just laughs and says he can't give away all his secrets. We lie in bed, passing it back and forth, sheets tangled around us, my head on his chest, still slightly salty with sweat, and I'm perfectly content. It scares me how fast I'm falling for him, given that I hardly even know him yet, and that we certainly haven't talked about anything like a future.

And then, on Wednesday night of our second week together, he tells me he's going away on Friday. "It's a business trip," he says. "To Vegas. Just for the weekend."

"Oh." I'm suddenly, absurdly disappointed. Two days without him—three, at the most—but suddenly the weekend, which I'd imagined spending lying in bed all morning, then going out for brunch and an afternoon walk, then sipping wine at some impossibly chic bar where all the men looked like Lewis and all the women looked like models (but he only had eyes for me)—stretches before me like a blank gray space.

"You should come with me," he says. And just like that my heart, which had been in a puddle somewhere around my feet, bounces back into my chest again. He wants to travel with me! To Vegas! I've never even been to Vegas, and somehow I have a feeling that Lewis would make an excellent guide to the City of Sin. "The hotel's all covered," he continues. "All you'd have to pay for would be your flight."

And then I come back to reality. A last minute flight to Vegas could easily be four or five hundred dollars, and I have exactly forty-four dollars in my checking account at the moment. I'm getting paid tomorrow, but that money's going into next month's rent. "I'd love to," I tell him. "But I don't think I can swing it. I don't have a lot of extra cash right now."

We're in my living room, sitting on the camel-colored leather sofa Nat bought when she and Melissa first moved into the apartment, a year and a half before Ben and I broke up and I moved in with them. It's Lewis' first time over at my place. Nat and Mel insisted they *had* to meet him, so Mel told me to bring him over and she'd cook dinner for all of us. (Did I mention that she's also practically a gourmet chef?) But Mel got stuck working late at the office, and Nat's waiting in a long line at an "*amazing*" DVF sample sale, so Lewis and I are waiting for the girls to get home.

On the coffee table in front of us is the latest issue of *Vogue*, and stuck in between the glossy pink and green pages as a bookmark is a stack of hundred dollar bills. Lewis' eye falls on the money. "What about that?" he says.

"Oh," I chuckle. "That's not mine, it's Natalie's." Nat sometimes gets paid in cash for her modeling jobs, and she tends to be careless about money, leaving bills lying around all over the apartment. I once found two dripping wet hundreds as I was emptying the dishwasher.

"Okay," he says, "but didn't you say she's rich?"

"Um, yeah," I tell him. "But . . ."

"So you really think she'd notice if a few of them were gone?" He gives me a sideways smile, his wicked smile, and I can't tell if he's joking. He has to be joking . . . right?

"Um . . ." I chuckle uncomfortably.

"Seriously," he says. "She wouldn't know the difference, and you'd get to go to Vegas . . . with me."

Maybe he isn't joking. And for a brief moment I actually let myself consider it . . . Lewis in a tux and me in a shimmery gold evening gown—not that I actually have a shimmery gold evening gown, but it's a fantasy, right?—sipping champagne and watching him win at blackjack before we go dancing at Tao or Pure or some other place I've read about in gossip magazines.

Natalie really *wouldn't* know the difference. When I'd handed her the hundred-dollar bills I'd found in the dishwasher, she'd just blinked in surprise and said thank you. She'd clearly had no idea they were even gone. And it's not as if she has to work for her money. Most of it comes from her dad's estate, and even when she has a modeling job, she's just standing there posing while people look at her, which is pretty much her favorite thing to do anyhow. But . . .

"I can't," I tell him.

"Why not?"

"I just . . . can't. It wouldn't be right."

Just then Melissa comes through the door, weighed down by a heavy black leather Kate Spade bag and a pile of documents in her arms. Lewis moves smoothly to the door to catch the teetering stack of documents, which are about to fall all over the floor, and then there are handshakes and introductions, and more handshakes and introductions when Nat comes breezing through the door a few minutes later, carrying five shopping bags with bright, gauzy scraps of fabric peeking out of them.

And then there's salmon with baby asparagus and a bottle of Sauvignon blanc, which Lewis brought to thank Mel for the dinner. And there's warm chocolate cake and laughter and conversation, and the girls are completely charmed by Lewis, just as I knew they would be. And finally after dessert, Nat and Mel tactfully retire to their own rooms, allowing Lewis and me to tactfully retire to my closet.

I'm embarrassed to show him my makeshift room, especially since his apartment looks like something out of the Waldorf Astoria. There's hardly any space to stand between the end of my full-size bed and the door, and my entire wardrobe is hanging from a bar next to the bed that runs along the wall (no room for a dresser). At least I've got a cute yellow and white striped bedspread (from Target, but Lewis doesn't need to know that), and a nice framed print of Central Park hanging above the bed.

I switch on the lamp in the corner of the closet, and it floods the tiny room with warm light. I shrug, giving Lewis a sheepish smile. "I told you it was small."

"It's cozy," he says, and he squeezes my shoulder. "I like it." And I can tell from his smile—not the wicked sideways smile, but a warm smile, his blue eyes crinkling up at the corners—that he really does. I turn the lamp down to low and step forward to kiss him, and we tumble together onto my bed, and soon our clothes are tossed in the corner—well, except for his socks—and my legs are wrapped around his and my mouth is pressed against his neck to keep from waking Mel and Nat up.

And then we drift off to sleep, his arm draped protectively across my chest in the darkness. Just as I'm falling asleep, I remember him looking at the money on the coffee table, saying: "She wouldn't know the difference." The Lewis who'd said that seemed like a completely different person than the one who'd complimented Nat's jewelry and Mel's cooking at dinner, who'd made me feel good about my tiny room. I decide to think about it in the morning.

# – 6 –

OF COURSE, I don't think about it in the morning. In the morning, Lewis and I have a repeat of the night before, and then I jump in a quick shower and rush off with wet hair to work. Which is busy—we have a meeting with Kruger coming up, so we have to put together a progress report of all the press we've gotten since the last time we saw them—and then after work Lewis calls and tells me to meet him at a tiny little pizza place in the Village, and after pizza with prosciutto and pecorino we spend the night at his apartment, and then he kisses me goodbye in the morning and tells me he'll see me Sunday.

He doesn't mention me coming with him again, and in fact, I don't think about it until that night, Friday night, when Nat and I are sitting in a booth at an Irish pub called McSwigger's. Mel's out of town—she's running the Marine Corps half-marathon with Brandon in D.C. this weekend. Not that she'd be caught dead at this place even if she were here . . . it's got sticky floors, tables with the names of years of drunk college students carved into them, and giant plastic shamrocks and Guinness signs on the walls.

But Nat's sleeping with Jimmy, one of the bartenders, and she's assured me that he'll give us our beers for free. This being the case, I've had a couple, as has Nat—and Jimmy, who's blond and Irish-looking and very cute—though not as cute as Lewis, I tell myself smugly—has brought a round of kamikaze shots over to our table also.

So we're both a little drunk, and, as we tend to do when we get a little drunk, we're talking about sex. It starts with Nat leaning across the table and confiding in a whisper that Jimmy has a tiny penis—she measures against the candle in a glass jar that sits on the table, and we both dissolve into giggles. Jimmy looks over and gives Nat a hopeful wave, and she blows him a kiss.

Usually these dish sessions just consist of me listening while Natalie talks about whatever guy—or guys—she's having sex with, but tonight I can actually contribute to the conversation. "Lewis?" I say, and Nat leans across the table eagerly. "Amazing."

"Amazing dick?"

"Amazing . . . everything. I mean, better than it's ever been. There's just one thing that's weird."

"What?" I hesitate. "Come on, spill!" Nat insists.

"He never takes his socks off."

"*What?*" Nat collapses into giggles again. "You mean, like, even while you're *doing it?*"

"Shhh! Yeah." Heads—mostly male heads—are turning to look at us. When a girl who looks like Natalie shrieks the words "doing it," the men in the vicinity tend to get excited. "That's weird, right?"

"Really weird!" she says. "Have you asked him about it?"

"No . . . I'm afraid it'll be some kind of . . . foot fungus or something, and then it'll be gross and embarrassing."

"He was the perfect man," Nat intones in a deep voice, "except he had disgusting feet."

"Shut up." I throw a sugar packet at her. She retaliates by tossing the entire salt shaker across the table at me. I scream and duck out of the way, and the salt shaker bounces off the bench and rolls under the table.

Now more people are looking at us, including Nat's bartender, Jimmy. "Sorry!" she mouths, and he hurries over to retrieve the salt shaker and bring us two more kamikazes, which we clink together and gulp down.

And then suddenly I'm thinking about Lewis and the money again. I probably wouldn't tell Nat about it if I were sober—I don't want her to think badly of him—but I'm tipsy and we're already kind of on the subject. "There's something else that's weird," I tell her.

"Yeah?"

"He, um . . . the other night . . . you'd left some money lying on the coffee table, and he—he wanted me to take it."

Her perfect black brows crinkle together. "Why?"

"He wanted me to come to Vegas this weekend, and I told him I couldn't afford it, and he—he wanted me to take the money to pay for a plane ticket. I didn't!" I add quickly. "Obviously. But actually," I continue, just now putting the incidents together, "that's not the first time he's tried to get me to do something . . . I don't know . . . something I felt like I shouldn't."

I tell her about how he wanted me to leave Linda, and take her only client with me. Nat's frowning, tapping her red manicured nails on the table. "So he's trying to tempt you," she says.

"Yeah, I—I guess. But what's the point?"

Before she can say anything in response, Jimmy comes over and asks us if we want to come outside for a smoke break, and we follow him out to the tiny, ivy-covered courtyard behind the bar.

Outside, Nat and I shiver in our tank tops. Jimmy hands each of us a cigarette, and I idly touch my finger to the tip, to see if I can make it light the way Lewis does. "What are you doing, Luce?" Nat asks me.

"Oh," I giggle. "It's this thing Lewis can do. He can light cigarettes without a lighter—just by touching them. But I can't do it." I touch my finger to the tip and giggle again.

Suddenly Nat's face changes. "Oh my God, Lucy," she exclaims. She drops her unlit cigarette on the ground, takes mine out of my mouth, and grabs me by the wrist, pulling me inside. Jimmy stares after us in bewilderment.

Inside the bar, she pulls me into the tiny bathroom, smelling of urine and covered with graffiti, and locks the door behind us. "I just figured out what it is about Lewis," she says.

"Yeah?"

"You're not going to like it."

"Okay . . ."

"I mean you're really not going to like it." She takes a deep, dramatic breath.

"Just tell me. It couldn't be that bad."

"Well, Luce," she says. "I think you're dating the human manifestation of Satan."

I burst into laughter. I'm bent almost double, clutching onto the edge of the sink, giggling. After a minute I get control of myself enough to look up at Nat, expecting her to be giggling just as hard as I am. But she's not laughing. She's not even smiling.

"I'm serious, Lucy," she says.

This sets me off all over again. "You think Lewis is the—the—" I'm laughing too hard to get the words out.

"The devil," she says. "Basically."

I think I mentioned that Nat's a big believer in the occult. On top of the weekly séances where she tries to contact her father, she's also got a big leather-bound book that she claims contains spells, and more than once she's driven Mel crazy by boiling up some foul-smelling concoction in our kitchen and then forgetting to clean the pot. So, coming from her, this actually isn't all that surprising. She once dumped a guy because she was genuinely convinced that he was a vampire.

"Think about it," she says. "He can light cigarettes just by touching them . . . and didn't you say he had a closet full of fire in his apartment?"

"He had a fire in the closet in his apartment," I say, finally getting the giggles under control. "It's different."

"And he keeps trying to tempt you into doing things you shouldn't," she continues. "Which is exactly what the devil comes to earth in order to do. It's like in *Faust*. Or, um, 'The Devil and Daniel Webster.'"

"I thought the devil came to earth to play fiddle in 'The Devil and Daniel Webster.'"

"No, that's 'Devil Went Down to Georgia.' 'The Devil and Daniel Webster' is when the farmer sells his soul to the devil in exchange for seven years of good harvests," Nat says.

"Oh yeah!" It's enough to start me giggling again. "You're totally right." We'd had to read the story in an American lit class we'd both taken our sophomore year at Cornell.

"See!" Nat says. "He's trying to steal your soul!"

This makes me laugh harder. "Let's go back out," I say. "This bathroom smells like pee." I grab her arm and start to pull her out of the ladies' room.

"I'm *serious*, Luce!" Nat says as I tug her towards the bar.

"Yeah, okay."

Jimmy is back behind the bar, pouring vodka sodas for two blonde girls perched on bar stools at the other end. His face lights up when he sees Natalie again.

"Jimmy, get her another beer," I tell him, resting my elbows on the sticky wooden corner of the bar. Ignoring the half-finished vodka sodas, Jimmy begins pouring Nat a pint of Smithwicks. The blonde girls wrinkle their noses in annoyance.

"I'm worried about you!" Nat insists. But just then "Build Me Up Buttercup" comes on the jukebox, and Jimmy, still ignoring the vodka soda girls, grabs Natalie's hands and pulls her behind the bar to dance. One of the blonde girls pulls out a twenty dollar bill and waves it at Jimmy, but he's got his hands on Nat's bare back, left exposed by the purple silk scrap of material she's wearing ("It *would* be trashy," she'd said happily when we were getting ready that night, "but it's DVF, so it's okay") and there's no way he's letting go. I look at the blonde girl and shrug, and she and her friend, exasperated, make a show of noisily slamming the legs of their bar stools against the floor as they climb down and head for the door.

Almost before the door has closed behind them, dancing has turned into making out, and it's clear that Nat is going to be otherwise engaged for the rest of the evening. I've had enough to drink anyway, and my bed is starting to sound really attractive . . . though not as attractive as it would if Lewis were waiting in it. So I grab my cardigan and head outside to catch a cab home. I feel sure that Nat will have forgotten all about our conversation by tomorrow morning.

BUT WHEN I finally get out of bed around eleven a.m.—I'm

making up for all the sleep I haven't been getting with Lewis—Nat's sitting on the couch with her legs curled under her, fresh-faced and dewy in a Cornell t-shirt and leggings. I know she had a lot to drink last night—more than I did—but she claims she doesn't get hangovers. "You wouldn't either," she says, "if you drank as much as I do. It's just a question of teaching the body to adjust." She's tapping away on her iPad, and she beckons me over to look at the screen.

"Coffee first," I tell her, and set a pot to bubbling in the kitchen. Then I come over to the couch. "How was the rest of your night?"

"Great!" she says. "After Jimmy locked up we did it on the pool table. He may have a candle-sized dick, but he knows how to use it." She sighs with satisfaction, then turns serious. "Now look at this."

She's pulled up Google, and in the search box at the top of the screen she's typed the words "human manifestation of Satan."

"Oh, no." I drop my head in my hands as she scrolls through the first page of search results, websites asserting that the human manifestation of Satan is anyone from Hitler to Boy George to John Kerry. On the second page of results, she clicks on a site called everythingsatan.com. Heavy metal music begins blaring from the iPad as an image of a red, horned devil against a black background fills the screen. "Nat, it's too early in the morning."

"It's almost noon," she says brightly, but she clicks the mute button on the laptop. The giant horned devil onscreen has faded, replaced by a banner headline:

## SATAN
## a.k.a. Lucifer, Abaddon, Apollyon, Mephistopheles
## Lord of Hell

My eye catches on the word "Mephistopheles." "Mephistopheles" . . . "Lewis Mephisto" . . . okay, that's weird. I'm about to mention it to Nat, but then I decide not to. She doesn't know Lewis' last name, and she doesn't need any more fodder for her ridiculous theory.

"I don't even think I *believe* in Satan," I tell her. I was raised Catholic, more or less—my family was of Irish descent, so my parents took my brother and me to church on Christmas Eve and Easter, but that's about it. Needless to say, on Christmas Eve and Easter there wasn't much hellfire and brimstone preaching, so I grew up thinking about God occasionally and the devil not at all.

In college I decided I was an agnostic, mostly because Ben was, and that's pretty much where I've remained. I'd be perfectly willing to believe in supernatural forces, whether for good or for evil—I just have yet to see any evidence that they actually exist.

"It doesn't matter whether you believe in him or not," Nat says. "He's out there."

Below the headline on the webpage are a series of links:

## Satan, Lord of Hell
## Satan in the Bible
## Satan in Fiction and Literature
## Satan on Earth

Nat clicks on this last one, and the screen fills with text. I sigh, go into the kitchen, pour my coffee into my favorite Cornell mug, and then sit back down on the couch to read it.

> Many people believe that Satan assumes human form from time to time, coming to earth to walk among us and lead us into temptation. Satan chooses vulnerable individuals and presents them with irresistible temptations, causing them to make decisions that will damn their souls to hell.

"Vulnerable individuals," Nat says. "That's you."
"Shut up," I tell her. But I keep on reading.

> So what does Satan look like when he comes to earth? "The devil takes many guises." However,

sources tend to agree that Satan can be identified by certain characteristics, most notably his cloven hooves.

"See," Nat crows. "Cloven hooves! That's what he's hiding!"

"You mean the socks?" I have to laugh. "Come on, Nat, that's totally ridiculous."

"I don't know," Nat says. "You've got to admit it kind of all adds up."

"Um, yeah . . . to something that's impossible."

"You don't know that. There are more things in heaven and earth . . . Anyway, there's an easy way to find out.

"What?"

"Take off his socks," she says. "Find out what's underneath them."

# – 7 –

SUNDAY NIGHT, Lewis sends me a text from the airport.

**Home in half an hour. Meet me at my place? ;)**

I'm sitting on the couch with Mel and Nat, watching a *Real Housewives of New Jersey* marathon. Mel's drafting a memo and doing crunches at the commercial breaks. Nat's painting her nails. I'm just watching TV . . . well, watching TV and checking my phone every thirty seconds to see if Lewis has called and I've somehow failed to hear it.

When my phone finally does beep, I snatch it up from the coffee table, read the message, and break into a huge smile. "Somebody's getting laid tonight," Mel teases when she sees my face.

"Who, me?" Nat says absently. She's absorbed in painting perfect white strips onto the tips of her nails for a French manicure.

"Well, probably," Mel says. "But I was talking about Lucy."

Nat looks up and sees me tapping furiously on my phone's screen. "Ohhhhh," she says, and gives me a significant look. "Well, just remember what we talked about."

"What did you talk about?" Mel asks.

"Nothing," I say firmly. Nat hasn't brought up her Lewis-as-Satan theory since Mel got home this morning, probably because she knows Mel would ridicule her mercilessly for it. Mel is nothing if not practical, and Nat's occult tendencies are alternately a source of amusement and exasperation. "It's been lovely, girls, but I've got to change."

In the closet, I take off my grey fleece sweatpants, pull my Cornell sweatshirt over my head, and slip into a pale pink lace bra and thong. I've always loved lingerie, even when I had no one to wear it for. I look at myself in the mirror on the back of my door, mentally cataloguing my flaws—my hair isn't quite turning under at the ends the way I like it to, my arms are flabby, my stomach is sticking out over the waistband of my thong. I resolve to get back into my habit of daily crunches again. I pull on a black cowl-neck sweater and dark jeans, then add black boots and gold earrings.

I emerge, do a quick twirl for Nat and Mel, then grab my purse and head out the door. I know I should take the subway, but I'm too impatient, so I flag down a cab outside . . . and end up pulling up in front of Lewis' building just as he's taking a small roller suitcase out of the trunk of a black limousine idling at the curb.

His back is turned, so he doesn't see me getting out of the taxi . . . and though I want to run up to him, I hesitate, because his face, as he reaches for his suitcase, is dark and foreboding. I wonder if he's angry at something . . . his brows are drawn together, and I've never noticed how sharp the line of his profile is. He exudes an energy that's almost malevolent, and for a moment, absurdly, I'm frightened. It occurs to me that I've never watched him when he didn't know I was there before.

Then he turns and sees me, and a smile breaks over his face like the sun coming out from behind a cloud. It's a smile that makes me see what he must have looked like as a little boy on Christmas morning. I break into a smile in return as I walk towards him, and he wraps his arms around me and kisses me lightly on the mouth. "I missed you," he says.

"I missed you too."

Upstairs, we start kissing as soon as the door is shut behind us. We tumble onto his bed, still kissing, and then he stops. "Wait," he says. "I got you something." He unzips the top compartment of his suitcase and pulls out a small, rectangular black box that says BULGARI on the lid. He flips it open.

I gasp. A beautiful diamond solitaire on a delicate gold chain winks up at me. I don't know much about diamonds, but it has to be over a carat. "Are you serious?"

He smiles, gathers up my hair with one hand, and fastens the necklace around my neck. I take a few steps towards the mirror. Lewis' bedroom is dark, but there's a faint glow from the light in the hallway, which the diamond seems to reflect and concentrate back up onto my face.

"Wow," I breathe involuntarily.

"Take off your shirt," Lewis says in a low voice from behind me.

Still facing the mirror, I take off my sweater. I can feel his eyes on my back.

"And your pants," he says. I unbutton my jeans, then step out of them. My body in the mirror is all pale skin and dark shadows. All of the flaws I'd noticed earlier are gone—I'm a sensuous silhouette of a woman, like something out of a movie, with the brilliant diamond winking around my neck.

"And everything," he says, and I take off the pink lace bra and panties, and then, wearing only the necklace, walk slowly over to the bed. I begin unbuttoning his shirt. I can feel him aching to touch me, but he keeps his hands at his sides while I push the shirt back off his shoulders, then slide the sleeves down his arms and over his hands. He remains totally still as I unbutton his pants, and then suddenly, with a groan, he pulls down the zipper himself, kicks them off, takes off his black boxer briefs and pushes me down on the bed, where he proceeds to render me almost senselessly glad he's back for the next two hours until we fall asleep, exhausted.

I usually sleep well at Lewis' place—his king-size bed has plenty of room for the two of us, and the eight hundred thread count sheets (I'm guessing, but they're the softest sheets I've ever felt) don't hurt either. But tonight my eyes snap open at four-thirteen a.m. The bedroom is dark, except for the glow of the city lights through the window, and on the other side of the bed Lewis is sleeping, his chest rising and falling with his quiet, regular breaths.

In repose, his face is peaceful and calm, his features symmetrical and sharply handsome. I spend a moment just looking at him, feeling a little shiver of remembered delight at the thought of his tongue on my skin. Then I roll over and pull the deliciously soft sheets close around me. Two and a half more hours until my alarm goes off.

But twenty minutes later, I still can't sleep. Something is bothering me, and as I'm absent-mindedly fingering the diamond around my neck, I realize what it is. A necklace like this must have cost more than a flight to Vegas would have—probably two or three times as much. If Lewis had really wanted me to come with him, why hadn't he just paid for my flight?—instead of telling me to take Natalie's money to do it?

And suddenly I'm hearing Nat's voice echoing in my head. "Take off his socks," she's saying. "Find out what's underneath them." Not that I'm actually giving any credit to her ridiculous theory. But I *am* curious about why Lewis wears his socks all the time, and just pulling one of them off would probably be a lot easier—and less embarrassing—than asking him about it. He probably wouldn't even wake up . . . he'd think he just kicked it off himself when he woke up in the morning.

And if he did wake up, and asked me what I was doing, I could just say I was . . . well . . . I'm not sure what. There isn't really a good excuse for taking off your lover's socks in the middle of the night to see out if he's got hooves underneath them. Except that's not what I'm doing! Because that would be crazy. And I'm not crazy. Just . . . curious.

I sit up in bed, lean over, and gently pull back the quilt and sheet from the other side of the bed. Lewis sleeps in only his socks and his black boxer briefs, and for a moment I'm distracted from my mission by the hard muscles of his thighs and butt, outlined in thin black cotton. He stirs, and I quickly lie back down and turn over, barely breathing, pretending to be asleep. After a few moments of lying perfectly still, I gingerly sit back up again.

Trying to move softly, I crawl down towards the edge of the bed. I'm on my hands and knees, my head facing Lewis' feet, and I reach out to grab the toe of one of his scrunched-up black socks and tug gently. It doesn't move. I pull a little harder, so that the toe hangs loose. Lewis' leg twitches. Quickly, I pull my hand back. He sighs, then settles back into sleep.

I reach out again, and my hand brushes against his foot. It feels oddly solid, less like skin than like plastic. *Plastic?* I reach out and tap one finger gently against his foot, and my nail makes a hollow clicking sound. Does he have prosthetic *feet?* Do prosthetic feet even exist?

I tug on the toe of the sock again, and Lewis' leg twitches in response. I pull my hand back. Maybe it would be better to do this all at once, like pulling off a Band-Aid. I grab the fistful of material that's hanging off the toe of the sock and pull, hard, and the sock comes off . . . as does whatever solid, foot-like object is inside the toe of it. And then I clap my hands over my mouth to swallow a scream.

Because his leg isn't . . . a leg, at least not from the ankle downward. It's tapered and slender, covered with coarse, brown and white hairs, like a goat. And instead of a foot, he has a black, split hoof.

I close my eyes for a minute, open them again, and the hoof is still there, resting on the smooth cotton sheets.

I can't—I can't—I have to be dreaming. I have to have fallen back asleep and be dreaming.

And then Lewis rolls over and opens his eyes . . . and sees me sitting there, hands over my mouth, eyes wide with shock. He sits up, blinking sleepily, and his eyes fall on his exposed hoof, travel from his hoof to my face and back again. "Damn," he says mildly.

# – 8 –

"I KNEW THIS would happen eventually," Lewis continues. "But I was hoping we might have a little more time first."

"I—I—" I can't even get any words out . . . not that I'd know what to say if I could. I just point at the hoof, my finger trembling.

"It's a hoof," he says. "The other one is too, in case you were wondering."

"It's a . . . cloven . . . hoof," I manage to say in a faint voice.

Lewis looks at me hard for a moment in the darkness, then nods. "So you've figured the whole thing out," he says ruefully.

"You're—"

"Yeah," he says.

"Say it," I say in a trembling voice. "I want you to say it."

He reaches over and switches his bedside lamp on, and suddenly the room is flooded with warm light. Then he looks back at me and shrugs. "I'm Satan," he says.

He looks so boyishly vulnerable, sitting there shirtless amidst the rumpled sheets, one sock on and one off, blinking sleep out of his blue eyes, that I want to laugh. Of course, I also want to cry. I can feel the tears welling up in the corners of my eyes, but I manage to keep my voice steady. "And you've been—all this time, you've been—trying to steal my soul?"

"Not *steal* it, exactly," he says. "Just . . . lead you into temptation. So that after you die, you'll end up going . . . my direction."

"To Hell."

He shrugs again. "Yeah."

"So if I'd taken Natalie's money . . . I would have gone to Hell?"

"No," he says. "That wouldn't have been enough, just by

itself. But once you get somebody started on the primrose path—"

"The what?"

"The primrose path to the everlasting bonfire. That's what the Bible calls it. Anyway, once someone gets started they'll usually go the rest of the way on their own. They start out doing small bad things, and end up doing bigger bad things, and soon . . ."

The tears are threatening to spill over. I blink rapidly. "So is this what you do all day?" I ask him. "When you're not with me, you're . . . going around trying to get people to do bad things?"

"Yeah," he says. "Basically. Although most people end up damning themselves to Hell all on their own. I just work on some of the ones who haven't."

"What do you mean, work on them?" I ask him.

"Start spending time with them," he says, "get close to them, get them to trust me."

And now a couple of tears do spill over my eyelids and down my cheeks, and I can't keep the quaver out of my voice. "Like you did with me."

He reaches out to try to touch my shoulder. "Oh, Lucy, don't cry—"

"Don't touch me!" I exclaim, and I'm off the bed and running out of the bedroom, down the hallway and towards the door, barefoot and wearing nothing but one of his white undershirts which I've borrowed to sleep in. I make it out the doorway and into the hall, and I'm frantically pressing the button on the elevator when he catches up to me, hobbling awkwardly on one hoof and one sock-clad foot. He grabs my arm, and for the first time it occurs to me to wonder what he does to people who've figured out his secret. Am I going to end up chopped into little pieces and stuffed down the garbage chute?

"Lucy, please," he says. "Can we talk about this?"

I struggle to pull away, but his fingers are digging into my skin. "I'm not going back in there," I spit at him. "So if you want to, I don't know, kill me or something, you're going to have to do it out here in the hallway."

He looks genuinely confused. "What?"

"Now that I know what you look like . . . doesn't that make me a threat?"

"Oh." He almost laughs. "No. It doesn't matter."

"I'll tell people," I tell him. "I'll send your picture to the newspapers."

"I'll just shift shape."

I'm so surprised I stop struggling. "You can do that?"

"I can look like whatever—whoever—I want. But even if I couldn't . . . Lucy, I'd never want to hurt you."

"It's too late," I tell him, and the tears start trickling out of my eyes again. "You already did."

His face twists, and he releases his grip on my arm. And instead of pressing the elevator button again I open the door to the stairwell and start running down the stairs, still barefoot and in his t-shirt, leaving my clothes and my purse and my wallet and my phone behind, blinded by tears.

I get to the bottom of the stairs, push open the door, and run through the lobby, ignoring the doorman, who half-rises behind the desk and looks alarmed. "Miss?" he calls after me. "Miss, is everything all right?" I pull open the heavy glass door and run out into the street, waving frantically for a taxi.

To my surprise, a yellow cab pulls to the curb almost immediately. I wouldn't have thought any cab would want to take a chance on picking up a crazy girl, since I'm sure that's what I look like, with my bare feet and my tangled hair and my oversized white t-shirt. But business is probably slow in the financial district at five in the morning. I don't have any money, but I'll figure that out when I get back home.

I pull open the cab door and jump into the back seat quickly, hoping maybe the driver won't notice that I have no visible means of paying him. "Thirty-Fourth and Third," I tell him, and he pulls away from the curb and starts driving uptown. The streets are dark and almost empty, and the city lights outside the window blur through a film of tears. I cover my mouth with my hands to keep in the small, choking sobs.

The driver glances over his shoulder at me. He's Middle

Eastern, in his fifties, with dark hair and a dark mustache. "Is because of a boy, right?" he asks compassionately.

"Yeah," I manage in a tear-choked voice, and then it occurs to me that Lewis isn't a boy, not really. "Well. Not exactly."

"Is because of a girl?" he says, his eyebrows lifting with interest.

This makes me smile through my tears. "No."

"Then because why?"

I'm not sure exactly how to tell him that it's because of the human manifestation of ultimate evil, so I just say: "It's nothing. Um, do you think I could use your phone?"

He takes a cell phone out of his pocket, and I open the glass partition so he can hand it back. I use the phone to call Natalie, who doesn't answer, so I try Melissa. She answers on the second ring, sounding sleepy but professional: "Melissa Davies." She probably figures it's someone from work.

"Hi, Mel, it's me. Could you meet me outside in five minutes with some money? I'll pay you back. I'm really sorry."

She tells me not to worry about it. "Is everything okay?"

"Yeah. No. Not really. I'll tell you all about it when I get home."


TEN MINUTES later, Mel has me wrapped in a blanket with a cup of hot cocoa on the living room couch, and I've started genuinely wondering if the past hour was just a nightmare. The living room is so normal, with its cream-colored carpet and dark wood coffee table and camel leather couch, and Mel, in her cashmere bathrobe, is such a calm, practical presence, that my discovery of the horrifying black hoof and the conversation that had followed seems completely impossible. It's the same feeling I've had when I wake up in the morning and remember some particularly strange or embarrassing conversation I had while I was drunk the night before. Only I wasn't drunk. And I know I wasn't dreaming. So I tell Mel everything that happened.

And, not surprisingly, she doesn't believe me. Well, she believes *me*, but she doesn't believe Lewis. "He's probably playing a joke," she says. "He's probably some sick Goth guy who gets off on this kind of thing."

"I, uh—I don't think so." The possibility hadn't occurred to me, but Lewis as a sick Goth actually seems *less* plausible than Lewis as Satan. "I mean, you met him. He's not very . . . Gothic."

"Not on the surface, but you never know about people. This guy that Brandon works with . . . blond and clean-cut as they come, but on weekends he likes to put on a teddy bear suit and go to Furries conventions. You know, where people dress up like stuffed animals and have sex."

I burst out laughing. "People *do* that?"

Mel starts laughing too. "The costumes . . . they have . . . they have *holes* . . ."

This makes me laugh even harder, but then the laughter turns into sobs and I'm crying again. Mel comes over to the couch from the arm chair where she's been sitting and puts her arms around me. "Sweetie, it's okay. It's going to be okay."

Just then, Natalie comes through the door, hair tousled and button-up shirt buttoned askew. She takes one look at my tear-stained face and drops her purse to the ground dramatically. "I was right," she says. "Wasn't I? That's an amazing necklace, by the way."

I put my hand to my neck and feel the diamond hanging there. I hadn't even realized I still had it on. "Oh, God. He gave it to me last night. I guess I'll have to sell it or something."

Nat opens the freezer, takes out a bottle of vanilla Stoli, and pours three shots into Columbia Business School shot glasses, part of a set Mel acquired while she was there.

"Come on, Nat, I can't," Mel protests. "I have to work in an hour."

"Lucy needs moral support right now," Nat declares, bringing the shots—and the bottle—over to the coffee table. Mel looks at my red eyes, shrugs, and takes her shot glass. We clink them together and toss them back. The vodka burns, then leaves a sickly sweet vanilla aftertaste. I slam my glass down on the coffee table.

"Another!" I demand, and Nat pours another shot for me and one for her—Mel puts her hand over the rim of her glass.

"I need to get dressed for work," she says. She bends down to give me another hug. "I don't know what's really going on—"

"What's really going on is that Lucy's been sleeping with Satan!" Nat exclaims.

"Like I said," Mel says patiently, "I don't know what's really going on . . . but it's going to be okay. He's just a boy."

"He's just a boy who was *perfect!*" I say, starting to sob again. Nat pours me a third shot, and I gulp it down quickly, spilling some vodka on the cream-colored blanket Mel's draped around my shoulders.

"I guess it's true what they say," Nat says. "Nobody's perfect."

# – 9 –

AFTER ANOTHER shot of vodka, I decide to call in sick. I've only missed work once before, when a suspicious-looking piece of sausage pizza from Penn Station gave me such a bad case of food poisoning that I vomited seventeen times in twenty minutes. (Or maybe it was twenty times in seventeen minutes. It was hard to keep track and vomit at the same time.) I called in sick the morning after that particular incident, and when I came back into the office the next day it looked as though a small tornado had touched down right on top of my usually orderly desk—piles of papers, receipts from vendors, full-color photos of vacuums spread everywhere.

Linda explained that she'd been looking for a press release and hadn't known where I kept it—despite the drawer I'd helpfully labeled "Press Releases" on the office filing cabinet. After that I decided it wasn't worth calling in sick, and through strep throat, the flu, countless hangovers, and wisdom tooth surgery, I came in. Sometimes I wore a surgical mask, but I came in.

But I figure that the fact that I've spent the last two weeks having (mind-blowingly incredible) sex with *Satan* is an excellent reason to give myself a mental health day. Plus, I'm drunk.

"We should go *dancing!*" I slur to Natalie, reaching for the vodka bottle (I've dispensed with the shot glass) and taking a swig from it.

"I don't know, Luce. I don't think there's anywhere to go dancing at seven in the morning."

If there *were* anywhere to go dancing at seven in the morning, I'm pretty sure Nat would know about it . . . so I'm inclined to believe her. "Well, okay, we should stay drunk until tonight . . . and *then* go dancing."

"Okay!" Nat says, grabbing the vodka from me and drinking. Then she yawns. "I'm just gonna . . . rest my eyes for a minute." She stretches out on the rug in front of the TV.

My eyelids suddenly weigh a thousand pounds, and resting them for a minute sounds like a great idea. I lean my head against the arm of the couch. "Yeah . . . me too. Just gonna sleep for a few . . . minutes . . . and then we'll keep drinking."

"Yeah," Nat murmurs sleepily.

I don't wake up until mid-afternoon. A shrill, repeated buzzing noise is drilling into my skull, and it takes me a minute to realize that it's our intercom. I don't really care who's at the door, but I want the noise to stop, so I drag myself up off the couch, stumble over to the intercom, and press the "Listen" button.

"Miss O'Neill? Lucy O'Neill?" the doorman says.

"Yeah?"

"You have a delivery at the front desk."

"Okay. I, uh—I'll be right down."

I catch a glimpse of myself in our hallway mirror as I stagger towards the elevator. My hair is matted into clumps and there are dark half-moons of eyeliner under my eyes. I have a disgusting taste in my mouth, and a headache that's tightening into a vise grip at the base of my skull. I want to go back to sleep. For about a million years.

And then the elevator doors open, and standing in front of the doorman's desk in the lobby is Lewis. He's wearing a black pinstripe suit and a pale blue shirt that brings out the blue in his eyes. He's breathtakingly handsome, and he's holding an enormous bouquet of flowers—tiger lilies and irises and orchids—and, in the other hand, the black leather Coach bag—a Christmas present from my parents—which I'd left at his apartment last night. His eyes widen a little when he sees the pale mess supporting herself against the side of the elevator.

And I panic. Instead of getting off, taking my purse, and telling Lewis to go away like an adult would, I instinctively reach forward to push the "Door Close" button. I jam my finger against the red button over and over until the doors, with agonizing slowness, start to shut.

"Lucy, wait. Please, I can—" Lewis manages when he realizes what I'm doing, and then the metal doors come together and cut off the rest of whatever he was going to say.

As soon as I get back upstairs I sit down on the couch, pull my knees up to my chest, and start to cry again. Grey late afternoon light is coming in through the windows, draining the room of color and turning the skyscrapers to muted shades of grey and blue. In the mornings, all of the buildings outside sparkle in the sunshine like limitless possibilities, but right now the view seems hopelessly lonely. Being with Lewis had brought the world down to a manageable size, because he and I had been all that had really mattered, but now it's just me all alone in the middle of the big city again.

Of course, I know that I'm being completely ridiculous. I've just learned that the devil is real, and all I can think about is that Lewis isn't going to be my boyfriend. For some reason I think of a story Melissa once told me; she'd been in high school, but she'd been visiting some older friends at Cornell, trying to decide whether she wanted to apply there. It was the first week, and classes hadn't started yet, so there'd been parties every night, and on Tuesday Mel's friends had been planning to host one. They'd bought Everclear and Kool-Aid the night before, woken up early that morning to move the furniture out of their common room and get everything ready . . . and then turned on the radio and heard the news that a plane had crashed into the World Trade Center. When she told me the story, Mel said that one of the first things she'd thought about when she'd heard the news report was whether her friends ought to cancel the party. She said she'd felt terrible for even thinking about the party at a time like that, but maybe it was just human nature.

So maybe the way I'm feeling now is human nature too. Lewis as the devil is an abstract idea, and even though I know—I've seen the evidence—that it's true, it's still hard to imagine. But the fact that he's just been using me is concrete and immediate, and leaves a taste of disappointment that mingles with the sour taste of leftover vodka in my mouth. I'd suspected that someone like him wouldn't really be interested in someone like me, and I'd been right. I should have known it all along, and part of me did, but I'd let myself suspend my disbelief because I wanted to so badly.

My head is throbbing, and I get up, go into the bathroom and shake two Excedrin out of the bottle. I go into the kitchen and pour myself a glass of water from the Brita, then take it back to the couch.

Nat is still sleeping peacefully on the living room carpet, her face bathed in grey light and her arms behind her head. Maybe I ought to be more like she is. I've been trying so hard to find someone who actually wants to be with me, and that obviously isn't working. But the city is full of guys—every bar, every restaurant, every street corner—and at least a few of them would probably be willing to have no-strings-attached sex. And maybe it would be fun. Nat certainly seems to think it is. At the very least, it would have to be more fun than sitting here crying over Lewis.

I toss the Excedrin in the garbage, pour out the water, and pick up the bottle of vodka instead. I'm ready to toast my new resolve, but when I unscrew the cap, the smell makes me gag, so I screw it on again.

Instead I go over to Nat, bend down and shake her shoulder. She opens her green eyes and blinks sleepily. "Nat, hey, Nat, wake up. We're going out."

# − 10 −

WHEN I GO OUT with the intention of finding a man to have sex with, I'm surprised by how easy it is. Normally I go out with the intention of finding a man *not* to have sex with . . . a man that wants to have sex with me, a man that I can suggest *will* have sex with me eventually, but only after he spends a respectable amount of time on me first. It's a complicated game, trying to seem willing and available, but not *too* available, trying to find the right combination of words and touches and kisses that will say yes, yes . . . but not yet. I don't realize how exhausting it is until I stop playing it.

Nat and I shower, put on some makeup (I go heavy on the blush and the undereye concealer, since the combination of a sleepless night and vodka for breakfast have left me with an unfortunate resemblance to a corpse), and get dressed. I go for a black miniskirt, a low cut red silk blouse, and my leopard print heels, since I figure that's how a girl who's looking for a one night stand ought to look. And Lewis' necklace—I can't bring myself to take it off. I'm telling myself that it's because the sparkle brings out my eyes, and not because he gave it to me. Nat, of course, looks amazing in jeans and a dark green ruffled tank top.

She offers to call up a photographer she knows (yes, in the Biblical sense) and have him bring a friend, but I don't want a setup. I want to go out, hook a man, reel him in, and then toss him back . . . all on my own. So we decide to go to a speakeasy in the East Village called Death and Company. I've never been there before, but Nat says they have delicious cocktails and even more delicious men.

Just as we're getting ready to leave, Mel comes in, takes off her cardigan to reveal the lacy tank top underneath, switches her black work tote for a green silk clutch and her high black heels for a silver pair of even higher ones, and announces she's coming with us. She doesn't usually go out on week nights, but she says it was a long day at work and she deserves to have a little fun.

We're in the elevator when I realize I don't have a purse—and furthermore, that I last saw my purse on Lewis' arm in the lobby. But when we get off the elevator, the doorman beckons me over. "I have your purse, Miss O'Neill," he says, "And I have this."

"This" is the bouquet of flowers Lewis was holding when I saw him—an enormous armful of tiger lilies and orchids, bursting out of purple tissue paper and tied with a yellow ribbon. The ribbon loops through a plain white envelope with a card inside. I open it.

*I can explain. Let me try. Please.*

I crumple up the card and throw it in the brass wastebasket next to the desk. "Are you married?" I ask the doorman.

"Yes . . ." he says, confused.

"Take these home and give them to your wife," I tell him, and I grab my purse and head out the door, Mel and Nat laughing and clapping. My purse is a big black leather tote, not really right for the tramp-on-the-town look I'm going for, but going upstairs to switch it for something smaller would have ruined my exit.

The bar is all dark wood and dim lighting, and even though it's a Monday night, all of the tables and most of the bar stools are full. And just as Nat promised, several of them are full of cute guys, after-work types in wire-rimmed glasses and business suits, just-out-of-college types in polos and khakis, and hipster types in horn-rimmed glasses and skinny jeans.

I usually go for the preppy boys, but tonight I'm equal-opportunity, so when a shaggy-haired hipster sits down on the barstool next to mine, I ask him what he recommends from the cocktail menu. It's eight pages long, and full of drinks with ingredients like elderflower liqueur and appleroot bitters, so it's a legitimate question.

He tells me that if I like gin, then I ought to try the Frisco Fizz, which features fresh squeezed lime and grapefruit juices and something called Dragon Tears. I order one, and Nat says: "Make it three!" and waves her credit card at the bartender before I can even open my wallet. "I'm paying tonight," she insists when I try to give her money. The drinks are fourteen dollars, so I don't really try that hard.

Hipster Boy's turned back to his friends while Nat and I have been talking, but after I get my drink he turns back around and asks me: "Do you like it?"

The drink is delicious, fizzy and refreshing. "It tastes like a wine cooler," I tell him, "but in a really good way."

He laughs. "What's your name?"

"Catarina," I tell him.

"Hi, Catarina," he says. "I'm Steve."

And then we're off on a conversation about the merits of different wine coolers—he likes Seagrams, while I prefer Bartles & Jaymes. This turns into a story about his high school graduation party, where he drank eight and ended up peeing on the kitchen floor in front of his parents, grandparents, and five year old twin cousins. He's bought me a second Frisco Fizz at this point, and so I'm tipsy enough to find this story endearing.

Besides, I like his t-shirt. It's pale blue and vintage-looking, and reads: **"I ♥ Crack"** in giant black letters across the front. He's got shaggy brown rock star hair, black skinny jeans, and a striped wool scarf draped casually around his neck. He's cute, or at least on one-and-a-half Frisco Fizzes he is.

So when he asks me what I'm doing after this, I screw up my courage and tell him: "I don't know, but I'm pretty sure it involves you, a bed, and a pair of handcuffs."

I've never said anything like this—anything even *close* to this—before. I have to admit I'm a little surprised that the heavens don't open and strike me dead with a lightning bolt . . . or that he doesn't burst out laughing.

Instead he just blinks at me. "Um. Are you serious?"

I lean forward on my barstool, giving him what I hope is a seductive look, my breasts almost spilling out of my low-cut red silk shirt. "I don't know. You want to find out?"

And he leans in and kisses me.

It isn't like kissing Lewis. It isn't a kiss that makes me forget where I am. I'm very conscious that I'm in a bar, and it really isn't the kind of bar where you kiss someone, and Mel and Nat are probably watching . . . and I'm vaguely wondering when we'll be done kissing so we can move on to whatever happens next. It's like kissing everyone else I've ever kissed *but* Lewis, basically.

But I try to put my heart—or at least my tongue—into it, and after kissing for a minute he pulls back, grins, and says, "I guess you're serious." I've never seen anyone signal for the check so fast.

Outside, he tells me he lives in Greenpoint, so I give the cab driver my address. We make out in the back of the cab on the way there, and I can't help but compare it to that first cab ride with Lewis back to his apartment. It doesn't compare very well. I feel vague stirrings of desire, but nothing more, and by the time we pull up in front of my building I'm starting to think I'd rather just go to bed than go through with this. I have to work in the morning, after all.

But he's here, and I can't very well send him away now . . . so I take his hand and lead him through the lobby to the elevator. The doorman raises his eyebrows and winks at me as we go by, and it's almost enough to make me feel like the sexy siren I was in the bar again. I put a little extra swing in my hips, conscious of Hipster Boy's eyes on my tight black skirt as he follows behind me.

"I kind of live in a closet," I warn him as I unlock my apartment door.

"That's cool," he says. "I kind of live in a warehouse. I'm a photographer." He says it as if living in a warehouse and being a photographer naturally go hand in hand. "What do you do?" he asks.

I don't feel like talking about work, since that will just remind me that I have to be there in less than eight hours. So instead I pull him into the dark entryway of my apartment and kiss him. "This," I tell him.

"You do this a lot?"

"Every night," I lie.

"Really?" he says. "I'm surprised. You don't look like the type."

"What do you mean?" I protest. "I'm wearing leopard print heels!"

"I know," he says, "and they're hot. But it's not the heels. It's your face."

"What's wrong with my face?"

"Nothing!" he says. "It looks—I don't know. It looks sweet. Innocent."

"I'm not sweet and innocent," I tell him, disappointed. Maybe with practice I'll be able to do a more credible tramp impression. I lean in and start kissing him again, and, still kissing, we stumble into the closet.

Almost immediately he bumps into the bed. "Ow!" he says, and I quickly switch the lamp on.

"Sorry!" I tell him, as he sits down on the edge of the bed and starts rubbing his shin. I sit down next to him. "I told you it was small."

"That's okay," he says, looking directly at me. "It's beautiful." His voice is husky with desire, and the sound of it is almost enough to make me forget about Lewis for a minute. "Take off your shirt."

I unzip the side zipper on my red silk shirt, and pull it over my head. I'm wearing a bright green lacy bra underneath it, and he raises his eyebrows in appreciation.

"You too," I tell him, and he unwinds the striped scarf from around his neck and peels his t-shirt over his head. Stripped of his hipster uniform, he looks skinny and pale and very exposed, like a snail without its shell. I suddenly wonder if he's even as old as I am. And if he does this sort of thing often. And if he sits in his apartment and looks out the window and gets scared of how big the world is sometimes. I switch the lamp off.

"Come here," he says from the darkness, and I grope my way back to the bed and across it until my hands, and then my lips, meet his. We start to kiss again, and we don't stop this time—except for him to rummage through his wallet and pull out a condom. We kiss, and then we touch, and then we take off the rest of each other's clothes, and then we have sex, and it's not like sex with Lewis—it's nothing like sex with Lewis—but it's better than being all by myself in the dark.

Afterwards he pulls me in close and cuddles awkwardly for a moment. I pull away before he does, grope through the clothes on my clothes rack until I find a t-shirt, and pull it over my head.

"I guess I should get dressed too," he says reluctantly.

"You probably should," I tell him. "Unless you feel like going back to Greenpoint naked."

"Greenpoint," he says, and sighs theatrically. "It's gonna take me *so* long to get home." I'm not sure what to say to this, so I don't say anything. "I'm so tired. I could just go to sleep right here," he continues.

"Um," I say. "I have to work in the morning. And I can't really sleep well with anyone else there."

This is a line that Nat uses on a regular basis. Coming from me, it's a lie, of course. I love sleeping with someone else there. I love rolling over in the curve of someone's arm, feeling the warmth of someone's skin, feeling safe. Just . . . not with him.

He sighs again, gets up and pulls on his jeans and his t-shirt. "Well," he says. "Can I get your phone number?"

I make up a string of numbers, and he punches them into his phone. "Do you spell your name with a C or a K?" he asks me.

A C or a K? What? And then I remember I'd told him my name was Catarina. "Um. C?"

"Cool. Well. How about I give you a call sometime this week?"

"Sure," I tell him. "That'd be great."

He leans down and gives me a peck, then retrieves his striped scarf from the floor and wraps it around his neck. I walk him to the door, open it, and keep a smile on my face until I shut it behind him.

After he's gone, I fish my phone out of my purse, set my

alarm for eight a.m., then fall back into bed, still wearing the t-shirt, not even bothering to wash my face. I'm so exhausted that I fall asleep immediately.

# − 11 −

I WAKE UP tired the next morning, but I've gotten used to waking up tired, my nocturnal activities with Lewis having seriously cut into my sleep time the past few weeks. After a shower, a bowl of corn flakes, and a cup of coffee I'm feeling almost normal. As I'm finishing up the coffee, Mel staggers in, still in her bathrobe, her usually sleek blonde hair snarled in tangles around her face.

"Aren't you supposed to be at work?" I greet her. She's usually gone before I'm even awake.

"I was supposed to be at work at seven," she mumbles. "Coffee?" I gesture towards the pot, still half full, and she pours herself a mug.

"So how was the rest of your night?" I ask her.

Mel rubs her eyes. "I have no idea," she says. "I had six—no, seven of those cocktails?"

Given that Mel weighs about a hundred pounds, I'm actually fairly impressed she's even upright this morning. I want to ask her why she was drinking like that on a Monday night—she's usually so responsible—but I can't think of a way to do it without sounding critical, and I'm certainly in no position to criticize anyone right now.

"How was yours?" she continues. "That guy?"

"Yeah."

"Yeah?" She raises her eyebrows significantly.

"It was . . . it was fun. Kind of."

And it had been. Kind of. At the very least, it had kept me from thinking about Lewis—or, okay, from thinking *only* about Lewis—for an entire evening.

Mel runs a hand through her hair, causing the blonde tangles to stick up alarmingly in all directions. "I don't know how I'm going to make it through the day at work," she says. For Mel, calling in sick is not even an option. One of her coworkers was in the office the day after brain surgery.

"Drink some water," I tell her, "a lot of water." I pour her a glass from the Brita and she drinks it down.

"Okay," she says, "I'm gonna go shower and make myself puke."

I look after her, worried. She really does look terrible. Then again, she runs marathons . . . she's used to pain. I make a mental note to ask Nat whether she knows if anything's wrong.

After another cup of coffee, I head out the door to work. It's one of those clear, brisk October days that makes you feel like raking leaves or going for a long run . . . not that I ever actually do either of those things. I'm thinking about last night . . . it didn't make me feel bad, exactly, but it didn't really make me feel any better either. It didn't really make me feel anything. And I don't have any particular desire to do it again . . . with him, or with anyone else . . . well, except Lewis. I briefly fall into a reverie, imagining his hands on my . . . no. Not going to think about that.

As I climb the stairs to the office, I try to ready myself for the disaster area Linda will have made of my desk. The desk is a mess, just as I was expecting—crumpled-up pieces of paper, empty file folders with their contents spread around my chair on the floor, and—inexplicably—something that bears a close resemblance to a hairball. I use one of the crumpled pieces of paper to drop the hairball gingerly into the trash, then set about restoring the file folders' contents and placing them in alphabetical order back into the filing cabinet.

After forty-five minutes, during which I've barely made a dent in the pile, Linda comes in, trailing scarf, papers, two different handbags, and a TJ Maxx shopping bag stuffed with the outfit she's wearing to an industry function after work. "Hi, Luce," she says. "Feeling better?" I assure her that I am.

"I am *so* sorry about the mess," she continues, "I just *had* to find the photos of the Kruger KleanAction—*Parenting* magazine wants to do a feature, isn't that fabulous!" I assure her that it is.

"Oh, and by the way," she says, "there's something on your desk."

Something on my desk?

"A—I don't know—a box," she says. "It was there when I came in yesterday."

I plunge my hands into the pile of papers and dig through it until I feel the edge of something hard. I pull it out. It's a bright orange box, trimmed in brown, and tied with a brown ribbon. "Hermes—Paris" is printed on the ribbon in white letters.

"This is . . . for me?" I ask Linda. "You sure it's not for you?"

"Well, I don't know," she says. "It was on your desk."

I untie the ribbon and gently lift off the top of the box. Inside is the most beautiful silk scarf I've ever seen.

It's printed in a pink and orange and red pattern, covered with tiny unicorns and elephants and birds which are cavorting across the silk landscape and intertwining with branches and flowers. I reach down to touch it, and the silk slips through my fingers like water.

Beneath the corner of the scarf is a card in a small white envelope. I open it. *I miss you*, it says.

"Well?" Linda says from the inner office. "What is it?"

I pick up the scarf by the corners and go to stand in the doorway of her office. She whistles. Linda isn't exactly a fashionista, but it's impossible not to see how gorgeous the scarf is. "Put it on," she says.

I fold the scarf over a couple of times, then knot it casually around my neck. I'm wearing a simple cream-colored sweater, a black skirt and black heels. I look down at myself. Even without a mirror, I can tell that the scarf takes the outfit from boring to fabulous.

I have to send it back. I can't keep it. I definitely can't keep it.

I look down at myself again, admiring the way the colors complement each other. Maybe I can keep it?

"So is this from that handsome guy who's been coming by to take you to lunch?" Linda asks.

"Um. Yeah."

"Lucky girl," she says. "He's a keeper."

I try to smile.


AFTER A TRIP to the bathroom to admire the scarf in the mirror (it brings a rosy glow to my cheeks and makes my outfit look effortlessly stylish . . . would it send completely the wrong message if I were to keep it?) and another two hours spent digging out my desk, I finally turn on my computer and check my email.

*To: ILoveLucy32345@yahoo.com*
*From: Lewis.Mephisto@gmail.com*
*5:14 am*
*[No Subject]*
*Lucy,*
*This has happened before. Every time I meet a woman I really enjoy spending time with, she finds out the truth eventually, and then she can't handle it. I thought—I hoped—that maybe you were different, that maybe you could accept me for who I am.*
*—Lewis*

I minimize my email and work on a press release for forty-five minutes, and then Linda goes out to lunch with Abdul and I pull the email back up and begin composing a reply.

*To: Lewis.Mephisto@gmail.com*
*From: ILoveLucy32345@yahoo.com*
*11:54 a.m.*
*Re: [No Subject]*
*Lewis,*
*I know that you're just trying to convince me to start spending time with you again so that you can keep trying to talk me into doing something horrible. But it's not going to work. I can see through your lies, and no matter how many expensive gifts*

*you send me, it's not going to change that.*

I stop typing and hit the backspace button until the text of the email disappears. Too angry. Too hurt. I try again.

*Lewis,*
*This has happened to me before, too. Every time I get involved*
*with a guy who seems perfect, it turns out he's been lying to*
*me about something incredibly important . . . like he's been*
*cheating on me with one of his coworkers . . . or he likes to*
*watch gay porn . . . or he's SATAN.*

I stop typing and start hitting the backspace button again. I need something that sounds indifferent. Firm, but indifferent.

*Lewis,*
*I don't want to talk to you. Or hear from you. Please do not try*
*to contact me again.*
*—Lucy*
*P.S. Thanks for the scarf.*

I'm not sure about the P.S., but it seems too ungracious not to thank him, since—if I'm being honest with myself—there's no way I'm not going to keep it. I hit the send button quickly, before I can second-guess myself again. I need to stop thinking about Lewis and concentrate on work.

Of course, this proves impossible for the rest of the afternoon, as I can't stop checking my email to see if he's ignored my request and written me back. By six-fifteen, when I leave for the day, he hasn't. By six-thirty-six, when I get home and log in on my laptop, he still hasn't. By eight-oh-two, he still hasn't, and that's when I decide that the only thing that's going to keep me from checking my email every five minutes for the rest of the night is to go out again. Mel has already staggered through the door, kicked off her heels, and passed out in her bedroom, but when I call Nat she's more than game. She tells me to meet her at the Blind Tiger in forty-five minutes.

Three hours and three microbrews later, I'm having sex

with a lawyer. His name is Jason—or possibly James. My name, for tonight at least, is Clarissa. Jason or possibly James has turned out to be an excellent kisser, and even better with his tongue below the belt, and Clarissa is enjoying herself more than she'd expected. It's still nothing like being with Lewis, but Clarissa doesn't want to think about being with Lewis, which is why she's having sex with Jason or possibly James.

Jason or possibly James lives in a loft in Soho with a huge plate glass window, and while they're having sex on his couch, Clarissa is looking over his shoulder and wondering whether looking out at the city lights while having sex with someone whose name she doesn't even know is more or less lonely than looking out at the city lights alone. She can't decide, but by the time Jason or possibly James gives her twenty dollars for cab fare and a kiss goodnight, she's too exhausted to keep thinking about it, and when she gets home she falls immediately asleep.

# – 12 –

WEDNESDAY AND Thursday nights, I stay in. I've done the one night stand thing—twice—and it hasn't made me stop thinking about Lewis. In fact, I'm thinking about him more than ever.

It doesn't help that the universe seems to be conspiring to remind me of him at every turn. I hear "Devil in a Blue Dress" playing when I stop into H&M on the way home from work, and "Hell's Bells" blasting from the window of a car going by as I buy a pretzel from a street vendor. A wild-haired homeless woman on the corner of Sixth Avenue holds up a cardboard sign that proclaims: "Satan Is Everywhere!" I want to tell her I'm pretty sure he's actually just down in the financial district. When I'm flipping channels Thursday night, I come across *The Witches of Eastwick*. Jack Nicholson makes a handsome devil, but I can't help thinking that he's got nothing on the real thing.

I'm not sure how to stop thinking incessantly about Lewis, but clearly sleeping with strangers is not the answer. So I figure I'll stay in Friday night, too . . . it's been a long day at work, it's raining, and spending the evening on the couch watching *Casablanca*, which arrived from Netflix three weeks ago and has been sitting on the kitchen counter ever since, sounds more appealing than squeezing myself into an uncomfortable shirt and even more uncomfortable shoes and hitting the town.

But of course, Natalie's having none of it. As soon as I walk in the door she jumps up off the couch and hands me a shot glass full of tequila. Another is waiting on the coffee table for Mel.

"It's *really* good," she says. "Ron went to Mexico last week, and he brought this back for me."

"Ron." I search through my mental files. "Is he the pilot, or the engineer?"

"Neither one," she says. "He's the psychologist."

"You're sleeping with your psychologist?"

"No!" she exclaims, and takes a swallow of tequila straight from the tiny, bright blue bottle. Halfway through, she puts up her finger as if she's just remembered something. "Wait, yes. I did once. But it was a long time ago."

"Natalie!"

"What?" she says innocently. "Sex can be very therapeutic. Anyway, Ron's not *my* psychologist. He's a different psychologist. We met at a party a couple of weeks ago, and we did it in the bathroom, and he's been calling me non-stop ever since, which is annoying. But this tequila almost makes up for it." She grabs the bottle and takes another gulp. "Try some."

The smell of the tequila is faintly nauseating, and I set my full shot glass back down. "I don't think so," I tell her. "I'm going to stay in tonight."

"Nooooo!" Nat wails. "You can't! There's like six amazing parties we have to go to!"

Just then, Mel comes in the door, dropping her heavy black bag on the kitchen counter. I've hardly seen her all week. But I figure she's just been working late—that or staying over at Brandon's. She comes into the living room, and sees the shot glasses sitting on the coffee table. "Tequila?"

"Awesome tequila," Nat says.

"Awesome." Mel grabs her glass, tosses it back, then grabs mine and drinks that one too. "So where are we going tonight?"

"Everywhere," Nat says. "Except Lucy is being a loser and saying she doesn't want to come."

"Come on!" Mel says. "You have to go out on Friday night!"

"Pleeeeeaaaaase," Nat wheedles. "I'll let you carry my baby Gucci."

Nat's "baby Gucci" is a tiny black sequined clutch, barely large enough to hold a lipstick and a credit card, which cost two thousand dollars. I covet it desperately.

"And I'll do your makeup," Mel says. "I'll give you really

smoky eyes."

"Fine," I tell them. "I'll go out. But I'm *not* drinking any tequila."

"It doesn't matter," Nat says. "It's almost gone anyhow." She pours the dregs of the tiny bottle into two of the shot glasses, and she and Mel toss the shots back.

"Wait!" Mel says. "I've got something even better." She goes into the kitchen, rummages in the back of the fridge, and comes out with a bottle of Dom Perignon.

"Wait a minute," I say, "isn't that the bottle you and Brandon are saving for your engagement party?" They got engaged in August, but they want to have the party at Le Cirque, and the first date they could book it was in December.

"It's all right," she says. "We can buy another one or something."

She pops the cork and it goes flying across the living room, narrowly missing Natalie's head. Nat shrieks, and champagne begins spilling out of the bottle onto the carpet. Quickly, Mel tips the bottle back into her mouth and drinks until it stops fizzing. "Whew!" she exclaims. "Glasses?"

Nat runs into the kitchen and grabs three champagne flutes. "Um. Are you sure you want to drink your engagement champagne tonight?" I ask Mel.

"Well, it's open, so now we have to," she replies cheerfully, and pours it into the glasses. I don't know much about champagne, but even I can tell this is delicious—fizzy and tart, each bubble seeming to pop individually on the tongue.

An hour later, smoky eye makeup applied and Nat's baby Gucci clutched firmly in hand, I'm sitting at the bar at Vinoteca. We've decided to stop in here to get a bite to eat before we hit the town. I'm still (mostly) sober, having had only a glass of champagne at the house and half a glass of wine at the bar, when a guy in a suit comes over to invite Natalie—"and your friends"—to join him and his friends at their table.

There are three of them—all stockbrokers, all wearing suits—and they have a few plates of appetizers and a couple of bottles of chianti. The one closest to me has short brown hair and blue eyes and reminds me a little of Lewis, which is probably why I smile and bat my eyes at him when he offers me a glass of wine. I make it through about half the glass, laughing and flirting with the brown-haired stockbroker, and then . . . well, and then I don't remember anything for the rest of the night.

Mel and Nat tell me the next day that they feel terrible for not realizing what was happening. They tell me I grabbed the stockbroker and told him to dance with me, but since there were too many tables and chairs in the way (it being, after all, a wine bar and not a disco), I climbed up on top of one of the tables and started dancing on it. And then I took off my shirt and started whipping it in circles around my head . . . which was the point at which management politely asked me to leave.

They tell me they tried to take me home, but I literally beat them off with my fists, insisting I was going home with the stockbroker. They asked me a couple of times if I was sure that was what I wanted to do, and when I said yes, they made sure he got me into a cab, then went back inside to finish off the bottle of chianti.

As for me . . . the next morning, I wake up in a bed that I immediately realize is not my own. For one thing, it's a king, and my closet can only accommodate a full. For another thing, the sheets are black, not white. And also, there's a half-naked, brown-haired man sleeping next to me. He's turned away, so I can't see his face, but I figure it's got to be the guy I vaguely remember flirting with at the wine bar last night. But why can't I remember anything else that happened?

And then he rolls over, still sleeping, and I see that it's not the stockbroker from the wine bar. It's Lewis.

# – 13 –

AS SOON AS I see him, the rest of his bedroom comes into focus—black sheets, teak bedposts, giant plate glass window with a view of lower Manhattan—and I wonder why I didn't recognize it before. I've certainly woken up here enough times . . . though I have no idea how I came to do so on this particular morning.

Maybe I called him when I was drunk last night? But I'd deleted his number, and no matter how drunk I was (extremely, judging by my complete lack of recollection, though I can't remember having more than two drinks), I couldn't quite believe I would have done that.

Maybe we ran into each other at a bar and ended up going home together? That seems more plausible. But did we have sex? I look down at myself—I'm wearing the sequined silver top I went out in last night, though some of the sequins have fallen off in the bed. My jeans are nowhere to be seen, but I still have my thong on . . . and my bra, I verify with a quick check. So maybe we didn't.

Well, whatever happened, it was a mistake . . . a *big* mistake . . . and I need to get out of here before Lewis wakes up. I sit up, carefully swinging my legs over the edge of the bed to the floor. I feel like I've been hit by a truck . . . and I look like it, I realize when I look in the mirror over the matching teak dresser. My smoky eye makeup has ended up smudged all over my face, my hair is tangled, and my skin has a sickly undertone of green. I *really* need to get out of here before Lewis wakes up.

My jeans, it turns out, are neatly folded in the corner, and Nat's baby Gucci (thank God I didn't lose it!) is sitting on top of them, along with one—only one—of my black heels. The other one must have ended up in a bar or a gutter somewhere. I squeeze on my jeans, button them, pick up the purse and the heel, and gently ease open the bedroom door.

"Lucy, wait," Lewis says from behind me.

Shit. I take a second to rub at the smears of mascara under my eyes and run my hands through my tangled hair, then turn around. He's sitting up in bed, shirtless, looking at me. "What do you want?"

"I just—" he says, and pauses, searching for words. "I'm not going to ask you to stay—or talk—or anything like that. I just want to ask you to be more careful."

More careful?

"If I hadn't been there last night . . ." he continues.

What *happened* last night? I want to ask, but I don't want to admit that I was too drunk to remember.

"I—" He pauses, briefly at a loss for words again, then shrugs. "I don't want to see you get hurt," he says, sounding almost surprised himself by the admission.

"Why would you care?" The bitter words are out before I can stop them. I don't want to get in a fight, I just want to leave . . . except that my mouth evidently thinks otherwise. "It's not like you care about me. It's not like you ever did."

"How can you even think that?" he asks, sounding genuinely hurt. "If I hadn't been there—what that guy would have done—"

"What guy?" I ask. "Are you talking about the stockbroker?"

"You don't remember?"

"I, um—" I look down, biting my lip. "I must have had too much to drink."

"You didn't drink too much," he says. "You were roofied."

"*What?*" But I suddenly realize it makes a lot of sense. It would explain the fact that I'd apparently been blackout drunk, though all I could remember drinking was a glass of champagne and a glass of wine. I'd never been too drunk to remember anything. "How do you know?" I ask him.

"I saw it."

"What? You were there?"

"No. It's a—a kind of power I have. I can see when people are about to do certain things . . . bad things . . . the kind of things that will send them to Hell."

"So you could see that he was about to . . ."

"Rape you." Lewis' jaw is clenched. "And I could go and stop him."

"You did that?" Lewis nods. "How?"

"Well, I went to his apartment—"

"He let you in?"

"No." He gives me a small, almost embarrassed smile. "I broke the door down. And then I picked you up and put you over my shoulder and carried you out of there."

I'm silent for a minute, trying to take all of this in. He could be lying, of course, but what he's saying makes sense. But there's still one big unanswered question. "Why?"

"Because I care about you," he says. He smiles again, and there's a hint of mischief in it this time. "You told me you care about me too, by the way."

"I . . . told you?"

"Last night. You were unconscious, but you woke up for a minute when I was putting you to bed."

Oh, no. "And I . . . said something?"

"You said *Hi*," he says.

"Oh." I'm relieved. "That's it?"

"And then I told you to go to sleep, and you rolled over and you said 'Okay. *Goodnight.*' And then you, uh . . . you said that you loved me."

"I *did?*" Lewis nods. He looks like he's enjoying watching me squirm with embarrassment. "Well—I don't. Thanks for . . . whatever you did. I have to go." I start to open the door again, and his voice, sharp as a command, stops me.

"Lucy!"

"What?" I suddenly feel like if I stay here another minute I'm going to start crying. I'm blinking furiously to keep the tears from coming into my eyes.

"I know that . . . you think I'm a bad guy."

"I think that's pretty much the general consensus." Him

being, you know, the *Lord of Evil.*

"But I could be good to you."

"Oh, really?" I demand, suddenly furious. "Just like you've been good to me so far?"

"I've tried to be," he says. "I've tried to take you nice places . . . get you nice things. I don't know what else you want."

"Maybe somebody who isn't trying to get me sent to Hell!"

"That's my *job*," he says. "And okay, maybe it started out that way . . . but as we started spending more time together . . . I, uh—I kept catching myself hoping that you wouldn't take the bait."

"Why?"

"So that I'd have to keep trying, and it would give me an excuse to see you again."

"And what about if I had taken the bait? Would that have been it?"

"I don't know," he says. "I thought so, at first—that's the way it usually goes. I . . . work on somebody, until I get them where I want them, and then I walk away. But I don't seem to be able to walk away from you."

"Well," I tell him, barely managing to keep the tremor out of my voice, "then I guess I'll have to do it."

I open the door and start down the hall. In seconds, he's out of bed, wearing only his boxers—and of course, his socks—and coming after me. He catches my arm and turns me around to face him.

"Lucy, please," he says. He's so close that I can see his eyelashes, hear his heart beating, feel the heat of his skin, and involuntarily my knees start to tremble. I won't let him kiss me. I can't let him kiss me. If he kisses me I'll be lost.

He kisses me. I tilt my head back and part my lips, and then I'm moving my tongue against his, softly at first, then harder, biting at his lips, running my tongue along his teeth, mashing my mouth against his.

We don't even make it back to the bedroom. We sink to our knees, still kissing, and begin pulling off each other's clothes right there on the hallway carpet. My shirt loses a few more sequins on its journey over my head. He takes off his boxers, then hesitates at his socks.

"Keep them on," I tell him. "I don't want to think about it."

He nods, and leans in to start kissing me again . . . and for the next few minutes, I lose all restraint, all control, and all capacity to think about anything at all.

# – 14 –

A HALF HOUR later, we're sitting on the hallway carpet, both a little dazed, smiling sheepishly at each other. I've recovered my sequined shirt—now looking quite a bit the worse for wear—and my red lace thong, and Lewis is back in his boxers. And apparently, neither of us is quite sure what to say, because we're looking at each other, half-smiling, then looking away again. Lewis is picking at invisible specks in the carpet.

Finally he says: "Brunch?"

Which is when I realize I'm starving. I hadn't actually gotten around to eating dinner at the bar last night—apparently getting roofied will make you forget about things like that. And the thought of eggs benedict—warm eggs and thick, salty slices of ham on top of a toasty English muffin—is suddenly too appealing to resist. Brunch is harmless, right? At least considerably more harmless than what we've spent the last half hour doing on the hallway carpet.

"Okay," I tell him.

We end up a Trinity, a restaurant/lounge near the water. It's housed in a former bank vault, and it's a popular happy hour destination for financial types. It's almost empty now, though, and I'm glad, because in my wrinkly shirt, dangling half its sequins from threads and missing the other half, and my hair in a messy ponytail, I'm hardly fit to be seen in public. At least I'm not barefoot—I managed to locate the other one of my heels in Lewis' front entryway. Lewis, of course, looks impeccable in a crisp blue and white striped button-down, jeans, and loafers, and I'm sure our waitress is wondering what he's doing with me.

I'm expecting him to try to talk about us again, but instead, oddly enough, we end up talking about my childhood. I mention that my mother used to make eggs benedict for all of us for breakfast on Sunday mornings, but she could never get the hollandaise sauce to come out right. I was shocked the first time I ordered it at a diner because the sauce wasn't lumpy—I'd always figured it was just supposed to be that way.

So Lewis starts asking me questions about my mom, and then about my dad and my older brother Jim, and soon I'm telling him stories—about how my dad, who was a classically trained tenor before he became a CPA, used to sing arias from famous operas while he was making dinner, but he'd always put in the family dog's name instead of whatever beautiful woman he was supposed to be singing about. About the time Jim and I took the car—I was eleven, and he was fifteen—our parents were out to dinner with friends, and we thought we'd drive downtown and get a slice of pizza. But of course, Jim literally ran into a police car that was stopped at a red light, and we both ended up grounded for a month. About my favorite teacher, Ms. Kittredge, who told me when I was in fifth grade that I had a real talent for writing—which was what encouraged me to take English classes at Cornell years later.

Lewis listens, laughs, asks all the right questions at the right time. I keep having the impulse to ask him the same questions—what about you?—what about your family?—but then catching myself. Even so, after two hours, when the remains of our eggs are congealing on our plates, I'm surprised by how disappointed I feel when the waitress comes by to give us the check. I'd forgotten how much I liked just sitting and talking to him.

Lewis hands her his credit card, waving away my tentative grab for my wallet, and begins putting on his jacket. "So listen," he says. "I've got this thing tomorrow night. Sort of a black-tie benefit—it's at the Met. A business associate gave me a couple of tickets, and I need a date. So do you think—just as a favor to me, I mean—would you be willing to go?"

A black-tie benefit? I've never been to a benefit before. Mel's gone to a few, because Brandon's mother is on the board of the ballet, and she always comes home with stories about sipping champagne with impossibly glamorous people like

Naomi Watts or Tinsley Mortimer.

But with Lewis? Despite the fact that he's just saved me from being raped—or maybe worse—I can't let myself believe that he really wants to be with me. If I let him back into my life, I'm sure that at some point he's going to start trying to tempt me into doing something terrible again. So I can't let him back in.

But . . . after all, there's not much he could tempt me into doing in just one evening. And maybe, like he said, he just needs a date.

"I understand if you don't—if you can't—" he says, seeing me hesitating.

"No," I say quickly. "I—I'll go."

"Good." A relieved smile breaks over his face.

"Except—" I say, suddenly realizing.

"What?"

"I don't know if I can. I don't—I don't have anything to wear."

"Oh," he says, "that's easy. Let's see—the event starts at eight. Meet me at Barneys at three, and we'll get you fixed up."

I've been living in the city for four years, and I've never set foot inside Barneys. Mel and Nat shop there sometimes, and I've stood outside, looked in the windows, watched the women in their fur coats, sunglasses, and tall leather boots push open the doors and stride confidently in. I can tell it's the kind of place where the salesladies would look at me and wonder what I was doing there.

"I can't buy a dress at Barneys—I can't afford—"

"No, no, no," he says, "I'll get it. You're doing me a favor—coming to this thing—it's only fair."

He'll *get* it? He'll buy me a designer dress? I have a feeling that I should not—should definitely not—allow him to buy me a designer dress.

But.

I mean, he's right. I'm doing him a favor by going to the benefit. And he's obviously got plenty of money—though I don't know—probably don't want to know—where it's coming from. And it's not like I can go to an event at the Met in my senior formal dress from college, which is stretch purple jersey with sparkles across the bodice, was purchased at TJ Maxx four years ago, and is the only long dress I currently own.

"Okay."

"Good," he says again, and holds the door for me as we walk out onto the street. I blink in the dazzling sunshine, so different from the darkness of the restaurant. Lewis puts out his arm and a cab stops almost immediately, and he opens the door for me. "I'll see you tomorrow, then," he says. He doesn't try to kiss me goodbye—which is good, because I wouldn't have let him—but I can't help but feel a faint, ridiculous pang of disappointment.

When I get home, Mel and Nat are painting their toenails fuchsia on the living room couch. "Hey girl," Nat says. "Where did *you* spend the night?"

"Um." I tell them the story.

Mel and Nat are properly horrified by my attempted date rape, but less than enthusiastic about the idea of my going to the benefit with Lewis. "Luce, I don't think—I mean, I *really* don't think—that you should be getting involved with him again," Nat says.

"I'm not getting involved with him again. I just want to go."

"I've been to quite a few of those things. They're really not that exciting," Mel says.

"Not that exciting? When you went to that benefit for the ballet last Christmas you told me you sat at a table with Ivanka Trump!"

"Yeah," she says, "but so what?"

"So I want to sit at a table with Ivanka Trump!"

"You don't want to sit at a table with Ivanka Trump," Nat says, "you want to sit at a table with Lewis."

"That's not true!"

Mel and Nat give each other a knowing look. "There's a lot of great guys in the world," Mel says, "and it just doesn't sound like he's one of them."

"Especially since he's *Satan!*" Nat exclaims.

"Or whoever he is," Mel says. She's apparently still holding onto the weird Gothic fetish theory.

"I know. I'm not getting involved with him. We'll go to this thing, and then . . ."

"And then?" Nat says.

"And then, that'll be it," I tell them. "And then I won't see him again."

# – 15 –

AT TWO-FORTY-FIVE the next afternoon, I'm standing on the sidewalk outside Barneys on Madison Avenue. I'm well-rested ("I got roofied last night!" having proved an ironclad excuse, even to Natalie, as to why I should spend Saturday night on the couch at home) and ready to shop, and the couture-clad mannequins in the windows, dangling bright leather bags from their white plastic shoulders, only heighten my sense of excitement.

But as I'm waiting for Lewis, I begin having doubts. All of the women going into the store are wearing heels and gold jewelry and enormous sunglasses with interlocking Cs or D&Gs or other letters that I don't recognize but I'm sure denote famous designers on them . . . and they all have shining, tousled blonde manes of Blake Lively hair. I'm wearing jeans and boots and a black hoodie from Old Navy—and Lewis' necklace, though I've tucked it underneath the long-sleeved thermal shirt I'm wearing underneath my hoodie. And even though I've blow-dried and flatironed my mousy brown hair, Blake Lively I'm not. Watching the shining heads going by, I find myself wishing I'd gone ahead and gotten highlights when I'd been thinking about it a few months ago. The two-hundred-dollar price tag had dissuaded me.

But then I see Lewis coming down the sidewalk. He's looking casually perfect in jeans and a navy blue Ralph Lauren sweater, and he starts smiling when he sees me. I start smiling when I see him too—I don't want to, but I can't help it—and we smile at each other until he closes the distance between us and leans in to give me a kiss—not on the mouth, but on the cheek. "You look nice," he says, and somehow I believe him.

He casually puts his arm around me, resting his hand on the

small of my back, as we go up the escalators to the third-floor designer eveningwear collections. I want to pull away—it probably sends the wrong message, given that after tonight I'm planning never to speak to him again—but it feels like it would be awkward. Besides, part of me likes the sense of being chosen. If a man who looks like Lewis wants to put his arm around me—even if his motives leave something to be desired—then maybe I belong in a place like Barneys after all.

And then we step onto the third floor, and the array of designer silks, satins, sparkles, and feathers spread out before us almost takes my breath away. "Wow," I say involuntarily, and Lewis chuckles.

"This thing tonight," he says, "it's going to be pretty fancy—so price isn't really an object. Just find something you like."

"Um. Okay."

I don't even know where to start, but fortunately a slim blonde salesclerk, with a French twist and sky-high heels, sees me fingering dresses helplessly and comes over to take us in hand. She sits Lewis in a chair outside the dressing room with a glass of champagne, and sends me into the room with a pile of dresses in rich jewel tones with labels like Azzuro, Armani Privé, Marchesa, and Azzedine Alaia. "Let me know if you need any help zipping anything up!" she calls to me from outside.

Feeling slightly dazed, I step out of my jeans, thermal shirt, and hoodie and into the first of the dresses she's selected, a long turquoise Marchesa silk gown, with turquoise beaded straps and a plunging neckline. It's a beautiful dress, falling in smooth drapes to its beaded hem, but it overwhelms me—I look small and pale in the three-way mirror.

The second dress is a sequined gold strapless Armani sheath, so heavy it almost stands up on its own. But when I try to zip myself into it, the dress bulges in all the wrong places, flattening my breasts but creating a roll around my waist. I take it off quickly.

But the third dress . . . oh, the third dress.

It's a coral-colored, Grecian-style Dior gown that brings

out the color in my cheeks. It's strapless, with a bust that gives me enviable cleavage and a bow underneath it that makes my waist look tiny, and it flows in beautiful pleats down to the floor. It's perfect. Lewis' necklace rests delicately in the hollow of my throat, and for the first time in my life, I honestly feel like a princess. Maybe this is how girls feel when they try on their wedding dress for the first time.

Lewis is on his iPhone when I come out of the dressing room, but he looks up and his eyes widen. "You look . . ." he says, and trails off.

"What?"

"I don't even know what the word is. It's a word that hasn't been invented yet."

"Um. A good word that hasn't been invented yet?"

"Definitely."

"So . . . this is the one?"

"I think this is the one," he confirms.

Just then the saleslady swoops back in—and stops short when she catches sight of me. "Oh!" she gushes. "You look amazing!" She goes on for a minute or two, but I'm only half-listening, feeling the heat of Lewis' eyes. My mind flashes back to the hallway, yesterday morning—Lewis pulling my shirt over my head—no. Not going to think about that.

"Okay," I interrupt the saleslady, "I'll go take it off now."

I go back into the dressing room, and (after admiring myself in the three-way mirror for another minute) unzip the dress and step out of it. And that's when I look at the price tag. Four thousand dollars.

Four *thousand* dollars? I've never even owned a piece of clothing that cost four *hundred* dollars.

Quickly, I pull my jeans and my hoodie back on and exit the dressing room, leaving the pile of dresses draped over the stool inside. Lewis looks at me, perplexed.

"Where's the dress?"

"We're not going to take it."

"You're . . . not?" the saleslady asks, her perfectly arched brows drawing together.

"Come here for a minute." I take Lewis' arm and pull him behind a rack of jeweled red Armani creations. "It's four thousand dollars," I whisper.

"Yeah," he says with a shrug. "I figured it was probably something like that."

"I can't let you buy me a dress that's four thousand dollars!"

"Why not?"

Why not? I don't want to get into why not. I just want to enjoy tonight, seeing as it's the last night we're going to spend together. Which is why I can't let him buy me a dress that costs four thousand dollars.

"Lucy," he continues, "if you haven't figured this out yet . . . money's not really an issue for me." I want to ask him why—where the money's coming from—but if he's doing something awful like embezzling from old ladies, I almost don't want to know. He must be able to read the struggle on my face, because he says: "It's nothing like what you're thinking. I—I'm a bit of a gambler, that's all."

"What . . . kind of gambler?"

"Cards, mostly," he says, "though I've been known to bet on dogs, horses, even a game of pool. And I happen to be pretty good."

"How good?"

He gives me the wolfish smile. "I won a hundred and forty grand in Vegas last weekend."

"A hundred and forty *thousand?*" I've accidentally raised my voice. Nearby, a blonde shopper with Chanel sunglasses perched on top of her head, Chanel ballet flats on her feet, and a giant black Chanel tote hanging off of her arm glances over at us. A miniature Pomeranian with a Chanel collar peers out of her tote, blinking sleepily.

"I've been doing this for a few hundred years," he continues. "Practice makes perfect. And of course, I . . . have a talent for reading human behavior."

"So whenever you get low on cash, you just . . . go to Vegas?"

"Or somewhere else . . . Foxwoods . . . Atlantic City. There are some beautiful casinos in the Bahamas, actually. Maybe we can go sometime."

"Um."

He puts a hand on my arm. "Lucy, listen. Let me just buy you the dress. If only so I can see you in it again."

"Well . . ."

He can tell I'm wavering. "Wait here. I'm going to go pay for it. I'll be right back."

I watch the Chanel woman shopping, fingering swaths of satin and lace, accepting a flute of champagne from another chic blonde salesclerk, of which Barneys seems to have an endless supply. What would it be like to be her? I can't imagine feeling like money weren't an issue . . . ever since I've been out of college and living on my own, it's been one of the things I've worried about. And before that I remember my parents worrying about it, heads bent over piles of bills at the dining room table late at night. What would it be like to shop at a place like this as if it were normal?

In a moment, Lewis reappears, holding the dress swathed in a giant black garment bag. "So," he says as we go back towards the escalator, "you're going to need shoes, right?"

We take the escalator up to the fourth floor, and after a few minutes I'm the owner of a pair of strappy gold heels that manage to be both delicate and astonishingly comfortable. "I think I'm probably going to wear these shoes every day for the rest of my life," I tell Lewis, and he chuckles.

Then there's a stop in the accessories department, back on the first floor, where I acquire a slim gold leather envelope clutch—it's Anya Hindmarch, a designer I've never even heard of. I don't even let myself look at the price tag, just nod in assent when Lewis asks if it's the one I want. I'm *definitely* going to carry this clutch every day for the rest of my life . . . every time I go out, at least. I love it even more than Nat's baby Gucci . . . the beautifully shiny leather, the streamlined, asymmetrical shape. I think it's the most elegant thing I've ever owned.

"So here's the plan for the rest of the afternoon," Lewis says as we head for the door. "You'll have to get your hair and makeup done—"

"I will?" I've never had my makeup done, and the only time I've had my hair done was when I was eighteen and a bridesmaid in my cousin's wedding.

"Yeah, you've got an appointment at Frederic Fekkai at four-thirty."

This day is getting more and more surreal. Natalie tried to book an appointment at Frederic Fekkai for six months last year and could never get in. "Okay . . ."

"It's only a couple of blocks from here. And I think the best thing would be to leave the dress with you—so you can get changed there, and I'll pick you up there in the car at seven-thirty."

"You . . . have a car?" This is the first I've heard of this.

"No, no, I just got us a limo for the evening. We can't exactly show up to a black-tie event in a taxi."

We can't? "Um, no. Of course not."

He walks me over to the salon, which is on the fourth floor of a building on Fifth Avenue. Inside, more Blake Lively look-alikes—in fact I'm fairly sure one of them is Blake Lively herself—are getting their tresses snipped, colored, and blow-dried by the black-smocked masters.

"Your appointment's with Claire," Lewis says. "I tried to get Frederic, but he's doing an event in Vegas. And Giovanni for makeup."

"Okay . . ."

"So I guess I'll see you in a couple of hours." He hands me the dress, and his fingers linger on mine for a moment. Then he turns and heads out of the salon.

Watching him walk, I have another brief flashback to the hallway incident yesterday morning—his hands on my hips, pulling off my thong, the look of desire in his eyes. I sigh and turn away quickly.

# – 16 –

THREE HOURS later, thanks to the ministrations of Claire and Giovanni—as well as Renee the colorist, Andrea the facialist, and Douglas the eyebrow guru, I'm completely transformed. Renee has given me honey-blonde highlights, which shimmer and catch the light, and Claire has snipped long layers into my hair to bring out the highlights and accentuate my cheekbones. Then, with the help of a curling iron, she's turned it into a mass of bouncy waves that frame my face. I can hardly stop tossing my head and running my hands through it.

Andrea has given me a thirty-minute oxygen facial, which has left my skin fresh and glowing (so this is why Mel gets a facial every month), and Douglas has shaped my brows into two pencil-thin arches that manage to make me look both delicate and surprised. And Giovanni. He's given me flawless skin, smoky eyes, and coral-colored lips that match my gown exactly.

The staff has graciously allowed me to change in one of the private rooms they use for facials, and has assured me that I'll be able to pick up my clothes at the salon tomorrow. So now I'm sitting in one of the salon chairs, admiring myself in the mirror, sipping champagne, and waiting for Lewis.

I should mention that I'm on my third glass of champagne at this point. They handed me a flute when I came in, and kept refilling it from a bottle of Veuve Clicquot while they worked on my hair and my face. Which, in my defense, probably explains a lot about what happens the rest of the night.

It starts out perfectly. At exactly seven-thirty, a long black limousine pulls up in front. I've been gazing anxiously out the window, and when Lewis climbs out, looking almost heartbreakingly debonair in a tuxedo that has to have been tailor-made for him, I can't help breaking into a wide smile. I

stand and take a couple of steps towards him just as he opens the
door of the salon and takes a couple of steps towards me, and
then we stop, gazing at each other for a minute.

"They'll have to invent a few more words," he says.

"I look okay?"

"You look like everything I've ever wanted."

The words hit me physically and take my breath away. No
one has ever said anything like that to me before. Of course,
Lewis is probably lying . . . but still. No one has ever said
anything like that to me before.

He comes close, until we're inches apart, and for a moment
I think we're going to kiss, can almost feel the heat of his lips on
mine. And then he takes my arm, and Claire and Giovanni and
Renee and Douglas and Andrea begin applauding, saying things
like: *"Che bella"* and *"Trop jolie"* and "What a beautiful couple."
And it's true, I realize, looking at us reflected arm in arm in the
mirrors over and over again. We do make a beautiful couple. Or
we would, if we were a couple, which we're not, of course.

It's once we're in the limo that things start to go south. The
museum is only a few blocks away—we could almost have
walked—but my "astonishingly comfortable" new Manolos
aren't exactly made for the New York City sidewalks, nor is the
hem of my gown, which trails on the floor. So we settle into the
leather seats, and Lewis opens the partition between us and the
driver.

"Could you go around the block, John?" he asks. "I want to
admire Lucy for a few minutes."

He picks up a bottle of champagne that's been sitting on ice
on the door, along with two glasses.

"Oh, I don't know," I tell him. "I had a few at the salon."

"So have a few more," he says with a smile, pouring the
champagne. He puts the bottle back on ice and lifts his glass to
mine. "Cheers," he says. "To a wonderful evening."

I can't exactly argue with that, so I clink my glass against his
and take a drink. My head is starting to feel as fizzy as the
bubbles in my champagne glass, and it suddenly occurs to me to
wonder: "Can you even *get* drunk?"

He chuckles. "When I'm in human form, sure," he says. "I can get drunk, I can get sick, I can hurt, I can get—" he runs a finger down my leg through the silk of my gown, and I shiver—"turned on. All the things humans do."

"What about . . . when you're not in human form? Are you . . . ?"

He laughs. "I'm not a giant red beast with horns and a pitchfork, if that's what you're asking. I'm sort of an elemental—like a wind, a fiery wind. Which is convenient for travel, but I prefer to be more substantial the rest of the time."

I try to nod sagely, as though having my date tell me that he was "sort of a fiery wind" were an everyday occurrence. "So . . . when you're in human form . . . you're just like a normal person?"

"Yes," he says. "Except I'm immortal, of course."

Of course. Also a totally normal thing for your date to tell you on the way to a black-tie benefit. "So you've . . . always been around?"

"Yes," he says, "and I always will be. In one form or another."

I take another sip of champagne. "So . . . you could, like, tell me what the world was like five thousand years ago."

"Sure," he says with a smile. "I could tell you all kinds of things."

"Wow." My glass is empty, and Lewis picks up the bottle and refills it. I take a sip. "So tell me something."

"Like what?"

I'm sure there are all kinds of intelligent questions I should be asking him about history, but after all the champagne I've had, they're not coming to mind. "Um. Did people really walk around in togas during the Roman Empire?"

"They did," he says. "At least free Roman citizens did. Slaves and foreigners weren't allowed to wear togas, so they just wore tunics."

"And what about gladiator sandals?"

"Only indoors," he says. "Sandals weren't considered outdoor footwear. Outdoors they wore shoes called *calcei* . . .

they were made of leather, sort of like boots."

"Cool." Just then the limo slows to a stop, and Lewis offers me his hand. "Are you ready?"

I feel like I could sit here all night, drinking champagne with Lewis, but I'm also curious about what's awaiting us inside. The driver comes around and opens the door, and Lewis takes my arm and helps me out, and arm in arm we walk up the wide, imposing stairs to the museum. My heel catches on one of the steps and I stumble a bit, and Lewis steadies me.

As we approach the door, it occurs to me to ask for the first time: "So what is this benefit . . . benefiting?"

"Multiple sclerosis research," he says.

"You support multiple sclerosis research?" I ask him, surprised.

"Why not?" he says.

Um. Because you're evil? But before I have a chance to reply, we're at the door. Lewis produces two tickets from a pocket of his tux and hands them to a man dressed in black and wearing a headset, who nods and gestures us inside. The museum's grand entrance hall is filled with people, all dressed to the nines, men in tuxedoes and women in sweeping gowns. Even with four glasses of champagne under my belt, in my four thousand dollar dress and with my new makeover, I'm dazzled. Waiters are circulating with trays of appetizers and drinks, and I grab a bacon-wrapped shrimp and another champagne flute as they go by.

"Is that—?" I whisper to Lewis, spotting a petite brunette in a midnight-blue gown.

"Eva Longoria," he confirms.

"And that's—" I whisper, seeing a face across the room that's familiar from hours of watching *Indiana Jones* movies with my brother, hiding under the blankets in my parents' bed during the scary parts.

"Harrison Ford," he says. "And Calista Flockhart." Calista is beautiful in a short red one-shoulder silk dress, but even more emaciated than she looks in magazines.

"This is kind of unbelievable," I whisper to Lewis, and he

smiles.

"I'm glad you like it."

"So where's your, um, your business associate?" I ask him.

"My what?"

"That gave you the tickets?"

"Oh," he says. "That was a lie, actually."

"What?"

"Nobody gave me tickets. I just—I wanted to take you somewhere fun."

My mouth drops. "So . . . you didn't have to come? You don't actually know anybody here?"

"Oh, I've met quite a few of them," he says. "But I looked different. They wouldn't recognize me now." He turns and looks down at me, and I lose myself for a minute in the blue of his eyes. "Tonight's not about business. It's just about you."

I pull myself away from his gaze, taking a big sip from my champagne glass. "But I'm business. Right?"

"No," he says, putting a finger on my jaw and turning me back to face him. "Not anymore."

He leans down and kisses me gently, a public kiss, a middle-of-a-hall-full-of-people kiss, but despite the glitterati milling around us, I feel myself responding, pressing my lips and my body against his. Just as the kiss starts to become deeper, I tear myself away again, suddenly blinking tears from my eyes.

"It isn't fair," I tell him.

"What?" he says, reaching out to put a hand on my shoulder. "Lucy, what's wrong?"

"I want so much to believe you."

"You can," he says earnestly.

"No I can't."

I shake his hand off my shoulder and walk away, still blinking furiously, searching for a waiter with more champagne. I'm not paying attention to where I'm going, just trying to get away from Lewis, and I almost walk directly into a man who steadies me with a hand on my shoulder. I look up. Perfectly tailored tuxedo, dark brown hair, starting to turn to silver at the temples, strong jaw, brown eyes. He's attractive. Older, but definitely attractive. And he's looking down at my cleavage, which Jeffrey has highlighted with shimmering bronzer, appreciatively.

"Sorry," I stammer. "I wasn't paying attention."

"Where were you going in such a hurry?" he asks.

"Just . . . to get a drink."

He laughs. "Girl after my own heart. Can I escort you to the bar?"

And suddenly Lewis is at my elbow. "No," he says in a steely voice. "I'm afraid you can't."

"Oh," says the older man, backing off, "I'm sorry—" But Lewis, fingers still gripping my elbow, almost hard enough to hurt, is leading me away in the opposite direction. Beyond the museum entryway, I see for the first time, the first hall in the Greek and Roman Antiquities wing is set for a banquet, tables interspersed among the ancient marble statues that are missing limbs from having spent thousands of years buried in the earth. The tables are set with white tablecloths and crystal vases full of purple flowers. The effect is magnificent.

Lewis pulls me behind a pedestal, on top of which is mounted a muscular headless torso, still bearing chisel scars. "Okay, Luce," he says. "We need to talk."

"Why?" I ask him, trying to shake his fingers off my arm.

"Because you persist in believing that I'm lying when I tell you I want to be with you."

"You don't want to be with me," I tell him, "you want to trick me into doing something terrible and get me sent to Hell!" My voice has risen, and a few of the people beginning to filter in from the main entryway glance at me curiously.

"Shh!" Lewis says, pulling me further into the corner. A naked marble woman gazes down at me from above with blank eyes. "That's not what I'm doing anymore," he says more quietly. "I promise."

"But how am I supposed to trust you?"

"I don't know," he says. "How are you ever supposed to trust anyone?"

"I . . ." I'm about to come back with a snappy reply, but I

realize I don't have one. "I don't know," I finish lamely.

"Every time you get involved with someone, you're making a choice," he says. "A choice to trust them, even though you don't really know yet whether you should."

"Yeah, okay, but most of the time they aren't Satan!" I exclaim, finally managing to pull myself away from his grasp and grabbing another champagne flute from a passing tray. I gulp the champagne down, set the flute back on the tray and pick up another. The waiter raises his eyebrows at me.

I tip back the second glass of champagne and drain it, then look around for a place to set the glass down—maybe on the base of the marble statue? I'm wobbling on my heels, and Lewis takes my arm again and gently plucks the champagne glass out of my fingers.

"Come on," he says. "They're seating for dinner. You need to sit down and have something to eat."

I want to pull away from him and walk to the table on my own, but the floor has started tilting at a distressing angle, and I allow him to put an arm around my shoulders to steady me and lead me over to our table. There's an elderly couple already seated, she in a beautiful, rich red velvet gown and he, of course, in a tuxedo. They introduce themselves as Mr. and Mrs. Jay Harrison and offer us each a glass of wine from the already open bottle of red on the table. I accept eagerly. Lewis gives me a concerned look that I ignore, then accepts as well.

Soon three more couples seat themselves at our table. Their faces are blurring together, but none of them appear to be anyone famous, which is disappointing. "How come there aren't any movie stars at our table?" I whisper to Lewis . . . or maybe I don't quite manage to whisper, because suddenly everyone at the table is looking at me.

"Just what I was wondering, dear," says Mrs. Jay Harrison graciously, and everyone laughs. Emboldened, I continue, waving my wine glass as I address the table.

"I mean, isn't that why people come to these things? To hang out with famous people? It's not really because of multiple sclerosis . . . is it? I mean, does anybody here *really* care about multiple sclerosis?"

"Our son has multiple sclerosis," Mrs. Jay Harrison says, her voice considerably chillier this time.

"Oh! God, that's terrible, I—I'm really sorry." I'm trying to think of something to say to salvage the situation. Toasts always make people feel better . . . don't they? I raise my wine glass. "To multiple sclerosis! Um, research," I proclaim, and drain half the glass before I realize that nobody else is drinking with me.

I set the glass down. The room, which has been tilting back and forth slowly for quite some time, has begun spinning faster, and a wave of nausea suddenly rises up from my stomach. "I'm going to throw up," I manage to announce, before I vomit champagne and red wine all over my place setting.

When I look up again, wiping my mouth with my white dinner napkin, a circle of horrified faces greets me. "I'm very sorry," Lewis mutters to the table. "Lucy, we have to go." He takes my elbow, but I stumble over my chair as I'm trying to stand up, so he picks me up, heels dangling, and carries me out of the Greek and Roman Antiquities hall, back through the museum entryway, and out the door. My last thought before I lose consciousness, somewhere on the way down the stairs, is that at least I won't have to think about whether I should cut things off with him anymore, since after tonight I'm sure he won't ever want to see me again.

# – 17 –

THE NEXT MORNING, I wake up in Lewis' bed with an aching body and a pounding head for the second time this weekend. This time, of course, I have nobody to blame for it but myself. It's a Monday, and normally I'd have to be at work, but it's Columbus Day and Linda, thank God, actually believes in taking federal holidays off. It's a good thing, because even getting out of bed seems like an impossible prospect, let alone getting showered and getting myself to the office ... and I couldn't very well call in sick for the second time in a week. Though, speaking of sick, I can smell a faint odor of vomit, which seems to be coming from my hair.

I pull a clump of hair around in front of my eyes and look at it. Yes, there are definitely greenish chunks in there. I sit up in bed, and the world swims for a second, then steadies. I manage to stand up and make it into the bathroom, where I throw up again. This actually makes me feel better, and I'm able to get my clothes off and get in the shower.

I stand under the hot water for a long time, wishing I could wash away the memory of last night. I'll have to borrow some clothes from Lewis, I guess, since I can't exactly take a taxi back to my place in my four-thousand-dollar dress ... and then maybe I can go home and sleep for eighteen hours and try to forget this ever happened. At least I'm unlikely to see any of the people who were there ever again, since I don't exactly make a habit of attending black-tie benefits on a regular basis.

I get out of the shower, wrap one of Lewis' giant red plush towels around myself, comb out my hair and go back into the bedroom. Lewis, who'd been sleeping in bed beside me when I first woke up, is gone. I groan silently. Not that I'd been planning to see him again after last night anyway ... but I wish I hadn't made such a fool of myself that he didn't even want to talk to me. I would have liked to preserve my dignity, to leave him with an image of me looking beautiful in my coral-colored gown . . . not vomiting all over said gown, not to mention the tablecloth.

Besides which, I don't have any clothes to wear home. I open the top drawer of Lewis' teak dresser. Maybe I can just grab a t-shirt and a pair of sweatpants, and then drop them back off with his doorman after work tomorrow. But as I'm rummaging through the drawer, I hear his voice from behind me.

"That's not actually where I keep the cocaine," he says, "if you were wondering."

"Oh!" I spin around. "I'm sorry. I was just—"

"Looking for some clothes?" He holds up a shopping bag. "I was hoping you'd join me for brunch, and I figured you couldn't very well do it in that." He gestures to his closet, where my dress is hanging.

"You . . . were?" I'm dumbfounded.

He hands me the bag. "You're a small, right?" Inside is a pair of supersoft, heather grey cashmere track pants and a matching zip-up hoodie. I rub the delicate material between my fingers. "Oh!" he exclaims. "I forgot shoes."

"That's all right, I can wear my heels," I say automatically, and then catch myself. Am I really going to brunch? I thought I was going to walk away and never see him again. Then again, I also figured he was going to walk away and never see me again. And I can't very well not go to brunch if he's bought me an entire outfit to go to brunch in.

So twenty minutes later, we're seated outside at a French café called Pamplemousse. It's an unseasonably warm October morning, and my wet, newly highlighted hair is drying in waves in the sun. I've purchased a pair of oversized black sunglasses from a street vendor, since despite two Excedrin, my head is feeling like it's filled with broken glass and I can't handle the direct sunlight. Lewis tells me that in my tracksuit and heels, with my oversized shades, I'm looking very Mafia princess. I'm not

feeling very Mafia princess, I'm feeling very hungover idiot . . .
but I'll take the compliment anyhow.

The waitress comes over and we order eggs. I look down at
the table, its slatted iron casting interlocking shadows on the
sidewalk, and play with my napkin for a minute. Then I force
myself to look up at Lewis. "So I'm really sorry about last night,"
I tell him.

"I feel terrible," he says at the same moment.

"You . . . what?"

"I was encouraging you to drink . . . in the limo . . . even
though you told me you'd had enough already. It's like even
when I try to, I can't stop myself from telling people to do bad
things."

I'm stunned. "Lewis . . . it isn't your fault I drank too much.
It's mine."

"But if I hadn't given you that champagne . . ."

"If you hadn't given me that champagne I still would have
had three glasses at the salon and, I don't know, four at the
party? Which would have been totally sufficient for me to make
a fool of myself."

"Really?" he says.

"Yeah," I tell him. "I acted like an idiot all on my own. And
I want to apologize for it."

He smiles. "Well," he says, "you were very entertaining. I'm
sure it's the most exciting thing that's happened to any of those
people in months."

I can't help but smile back. "Oh, I don't know. They
probably see starlets vomiting all over the tablecloth all the
time."

"Actually, that's probably true," Lewis admits. "Although I
bet the starlets don't look as pretty vomiting all over the
tablecloth as you do."

"Um."

"Sorry," he says. "That wasn't a very good compliment."

"I'm just glad you're still willing to speak to me," I tell him.
And I *am* glad. I can't help it. It's so nice to sit here across from
him, sipping our coffee, watching the people hurrying by on the

sidewalk. Most of them are in business suits . . . apparently people in finance don't get Columbus Day off. I remember what Lewis said to me the first night we met—"everyone's lost, but they all look like they know exactly where they're going."

"So tell me some more about what the world used to be like," I tell him.

"Okay," he says. "What do you want to know?"

"Tell me about . . . the French Revolution." Ever since my parents took me to see a touring Broadway production of *Les Misérables* when I was in middle school, I'd been fascinated by that particular period in history. "You were there for that, right?"

"Yes," he says. "Right in the middle of it."

And I suddenly realize that maybe I don't want to know. If Lewis was there on the barricades, urging people to kill each other, spurring on bloodshed . . . "Um. You know what? Never mind. Let's talk about something else."

Just then the waitress sets down our plates: a ham and Swiss omelet for me, bacon and cheddar for Lewis. "Lucy," he says once she's stepped away from the table. "I don't . . . enjoy . . . human suffering, if that's what you're thinking."

How does he always know what I'm thinking?

"Knowing what people are thinking is sort of my specialty," he says, answering the question I didn't ask again. "But you're easier to read than most. You wear your heart on your sleeve . . . it's one of the things I like about you."

"So . . . if you don't enjoy suffering . . . then why do you do what you do?"

"I have to," he says. "It's my . . . it's my purpose. It's my job to keep the world in balance, to make sure good people are rewarded and bad people are punished. In certain religious traditions, they refer to me as the Adversary, and I've always kind of liked that idea. Because if you never get tested—if you never get matched against a worthy adversary—then how can you really know what you're made of?"

"So it's your job to test people."

"It's my job to test people. Some of them pass—like you

have. Some of them don't."

"So who decides whether they pass?—whether they go to Heaven or Hell? Is it you? Or, um . . . God?"

"I think it's God. But I can't be sure. He's never deigned to tell me much about how the whole system works. And of course, I haven't seen him in many many years—not since I—" He breaks off, looking a little embarrassed.

"Oh, yeah . . . didn't you . . . " I pause, trying to recall what I learned in my twice-a-year church visits as a child. "Didn't you raise up an army in Heaven against Him, or something?"

Lewis looks more embarrassed. "I did, yes. Back when I was young and very arrogant."

"And then He cast you out of Heaven?"

"Yeah. Though not personally. It was more of a flaming abyss of fire sort of thing."

Right, of course, that sort of thing. "So then you . . . what? Just went down to Hell and set up shop there?"

"Yeah," he says, "Basically. God created Hell to keep the world in balance, and He decided that since I clearly wanted to rule somewhere, Hell would be an appropriate place."

"So He just . . . opened up a flaming abyss of fire, and down you went?"

"Pretty much," Lewis says. "It was the first revolution in history . . . and one of the shortest. But I've ended up pretty happy where I am. I get a bad rap, of course . . . but Hell is necessary, just the same way that prisons are. Bad people have to be punished . . . so I punish them. Simple as that."

"Except not quite, because you go around trying to get good people to do bad things so you can punish them too."

"Most of the people that end up in Hell do it without any help from me," Lewis says. "I just work on the ones that could go either way . . . that haven't done anything really great, but haven't done anything terrible either. And even those . . . I'm only one man—or, demon, I guess—so I only get to a very small percentage."

"Aren't there . . . other demons?"

"There are," he says, "but they don't do this work—it's too

delicate. They mostly work down in Hell . . . doing administrative tasks, maintenance, keeping everything running smoothly."

"Huh." I look down, stirring the ice cubes in my water glass with my straw, thinking about what he's said. It's a whole different way of looking at things . . . not in terms of good and evil, but in terms of balance, justice . . . it actually makes a lot of sense to me. I don't know how Father Tom, the pastor at the Catholic church my family went to occasionally, would feel about it . . .

"Oh, by the way," Lewis says, "on a completely different subject. I've got tickets to see *The Book of Mormon* on Broadway on Tuesday. I meant to ask you last night, but you passed out before I got around to it . . . will you come?"

I shouldn't. I should tell him I have a work obligation, or plans with friends. But I don't have a work obligation or plans with friends, and *The Book of Mormon* is supposed to be hilarious . . . and besides, I'm thinking about Lewis differently after our conversation. It's not that I'm completely fine with what he does . . . but I'm not completely ready to walk away from him because of it. I remember him looking at me last night in the museum, telling me that every time you get involved with somebody new you're making a choice to trust them, even though you don't know whether or not you should.

"Okay," I tell him. "Sure. That'd be great."

# – 18 –

LEWIS AND I fall easily back into the pattern we were in before: spending three or four nights a week together, except when I work late or have other plans. We start watching *Breaking Bad*, because neither of us has seen it, and we watch an episode or two each night before we go to bed. It's just as good as everyone says it is, which worries me, because I know if Lewis and I break things off again I'll associate the show with him, and I won't be able to keep watching. Ben and I broke up when we were in the middle of season two of *Twin Peaks*, and I still haven't been able to find out who killed Laura Palmer.

I love the time I spend with Lewis, but I can't quite feel comfortable, can't quite bring myself to think of it as something that will last. Part of it is that there are so many things we can't really talk about. I keep running into conversational roadblocks, stopping myself when I'm about to ask a question. I can't ask him about his family, because he has no family, and I can't ask him about his childhood because he didn't have one. I can't ask him about friends, because he doesn't have those either, at least not here on earth. He tells me he's close with Asmodeus, Beelzebub, Astaroth, and a few of the other major demons . . . but after he tells me a "hilarious" story involving Asmodeus, Astaroth, a gallon of whiskey and the eating of a puppy, I decide not to ask anything more about any of them. And of course, he doesn't really consider any humans his friends, since none of them know who he really is.

There are people who think he's their friend, of course, or their business associate (or their lover?—my mind keeps whispering, though Lewis insists that since he met me he hasn't played that role with anyone else). There are people he spends his days with, talking, coaxing, tempting—but I want to know as little about those people as possible. I'm more comfortable with what Lewis does, now that we've talked about it, but I'm definitely not completely at ease with the whole idea.

Part of it, too, is my friends' not-so-hidden disapproval. They don't come right out and tell me I ought to stop seeing Lewis, but there's none of the "How are things going?" or "We should all go out together sometime!" that usually happens when one of us gets involved with a new guy. (Or that happened when Mel got involved with Brandon, at least—I haven't been involved with a new guy since Ben, and "involved" is not exactly in Natalie's vocabulary.)

Under the weight of their unspoken concern, I find myself blowing Lewis off here and there to go out with the girls, flirting with boys at bars who don't interest me in the slightest, just to show my friends I still can. Nat and Mel encourage these flirtations . . ."That guy was so cute!" . . . "I think he'd be perfect for you!" I want to tell them I've already found a guy who's perfect for me—except, of course, for the one obvious way in which he's not.

My dilemma comes to a head one Wednesday night, almost three weeks after Lewis and I have started seeing each other again. We're at an Italian restaurant in the Village called Mia Sorella. It's a classic trattoria—red and white checked tablecloths, old Neapolitan music playing, ham hocks and strings of peppers hanging from the ceiling. Our waiter is an effusive, miniature Italian man in his sixties, and as soon as we come in he takes my coat, pulls out my chair, and tells me, "Oh, signorina!—you are looking so beautiful tonight!" He turns to Lewis. "Is she not?"

I'm still in my work clothes . . . basic black pants, white tank top, blue cardigan . . . and the eye shadow and mascara I applied before I left this morning wore off hours ago. But Lewis smiles, looking at me. "She is," he says.

"She is your girlfriend?" our waiter continues.

"Yes," Lewis says, and at the same time I say: "No."

All of us pause, the waiter looking back and forth between us. After a moment, Lewis says: "No."

"I will bring the wine list!" the waiter says, and hurries off into the kitchen.

"You're . . . not?" Lewis says once he's gone.

"I don't know—I—I mean we'd never talked about it . . ."

"Let's talk about it," he says. "Are you seeing anyone else?"

"No," I tell him.

"Do you want to see anyone else?"

"No . . ."

"Neither do I. So that makes you my girlfriend. Doesn't it?"

"I . . . don't know?" I don't know how to tell him that I'm just not sure I'm ready for the title of "Satan's girlfriend." It sounds like it should be the sequel to *Rosemary's Baby*, not a description of my life.

The waiter returns with the wine list, and Lewis selects a pinot grigio from the Lombardy region. The waiter nods, smiles, hurries away again.

"Look," Lewis says after he's gone. "I mentioned to you—a while back—that this has happened before."

Lewis and I haven't talked all that much about exes. He knows about Ben, but just the broad strokes, no details. And I don't know if he's had other liaisons of the kind that we have. I assume he must have . . . it would be naïve to think I'm the first girl he's ever fallen for in all of history. But I haven't wanted to ask. I haven't wanted to know how his other affairs turned out.

"Not often," he continues, "and not for a long time."

"How long?"

"The last time was almost two hundred years ago," he says. "I was working in Prussia then, at the court. She was a countess—half-Russian—a member of the nobility. Her name was Tatiana von Vordenstam."

I'm already jealous. I'm picturing Tatiana and Lewis kissing next to a fountain in the gardens outside a Prussian palace, her flowing brocade gown nipping in her tiny waist, her hair a blonde mass of curls. Of course, I have no idea what a Prussian palace actually looks like . . . or what Tatiana actually looked like . . . or even what Lewis looked like at that point. "So what happened?" I ask him.

"I fell in love with her," he says simply, and my jealousy intensifies. I tell myself that it's ridiculous to be envious of a girl who's been dead for two hundred years. "It started the way it always does," he continues. "I met her, we became lovers . . . and I began trying to discover the temptation she couldn't refuse. Usually it only takes a couple of weeks—but she was like you, she was very good-hearted, very pure. After a few months had gone by, I realized I was beginning to develop feelings—strong feelings. She was unmarried, and I began to think about asking for her hand. She thought I was a diplomat—so I could travel around the world and continue my work, and then return to her, to our estate, maybe even to our children. And then one day I forgot to lock the door to my chambers, and she walked in on me while I was changing my socks."

"So what happened?"

He smiles ruefully. "She was very devout, of course, like everyone was back then. The idea of being involved with someone like me was completely unthinkable."

"What did she do?"

"Married her cousin and immediately moved with him to an estate in the country. I toyed with the idea of taking another form, going after her, trying to somehow get back into her life. But I knew enough to know when I wasn't wanted."

"I'm . . ." Jealousy is warring with sympathy now. Poor Lewis. Though the way Tatiana von Vordenstam had reacted wasn't all that different from the way I'd reacted initially. If I'd had a cousin with an estate in the country, I probably would have married him too when I'd first learned the truth. "I'm sorry," I finish lamely.

"It's all right," he says. "It was a long time ago. Anyway, after what happened with Tatiana—it wasn't the first time something like that had happened, but I told myself that it would be the last—that getting seriously involved with anyone was just out of the question. I have urges, of course, and there were a lot of women who were all too happy to . . . gratify them—"

"A lot of women?" I interrupt him. I shouldn't ask, but I

can't help wondering what "a lot of women" means.

"Well," he says, looking a little embarrassed, "for a while I thought that the best cure for a broken heart would be to sleep with as many other women as possible. So I made it a sort of project to seduce some of the most celebrated beauties of the age . . . or of all the ages between then and now, I guess, actually."

"Like who?"

"Oh, I don't know. Sarah Bernhardt, Mata Hari, Brigitte Bardot, Jean Harlow, Marilyn Monroe—and quite a few of the current tabloid fixtures, of course." I want to ask which ones, but he continues: "But I told myself I wouldn't get attached to anyone again . . . and I didn't. For almost two hundred years. Until I met you."

"I just—I don't understand," I tell him. "I mean—obviously you could sleep with anyone in the world—or the *underworld*—and you really want to give all that up?"

"Look—Lucy—I've been a bachelor, more or less, for thousands of years. I've had my fun. I'm ready to settle down."

"But . . . with me?"

"First of all," he says, and he reaches forward and lightly touches my arm, "you have no idea how gorgeous you really are. But it's more than that. You're a genuinely good person. Do you have any idea how rare that is?"

I'm momentarily too surprised by his assertion to reply.

"There's a certain type of woman who's always been very attracted to me," he continues. "For my money, my power, my status . . . whether they knew who I really was, or not. But the women I've always found the most irresistible are the ones who are the most able to resist my temptations. The ones who are sweet . . . the ones who are innocent . . . the ones like you."

The waiter is back, hovering above us with an open bottle of pinot grigio. He pours a sip into my glass, and I taste it. "It's delicious," I tell him. He pours wine into our glasses, and Lewis lifts his glass to mine, then pauses.

"So are you my girlfriend?"

"Um. Well. I guess so." I'm still not convinced that this is a good idea, but after everything he's told me, I'm not sure what else to say.

Lewis breaks into a wide smile. "She's my girlfriend," he says to the waiter, and the waiter's face crinkles into a thousand wrinkles as he beams.

"I bring you oysters!" he exclaims as he disappears into the kitchen. "Very good for the making of love!"

# – 19 –

THE NEXT EVENING, I'm talking on the phone with my mom on my way home from work, which is something I do every few days. She's asking me whether I'm dating anyone—which is something *she* does every few days—and I happen to mention that I've been seeing Lewis.

I don't tell her much about him—just that he's a recruiter ("What's that?" "He, um, he works in human resources"), he's very handsome, it isn't serious yet but it could be, potentially. When she presses me for more I tell her I have to go because I'm meeting a friend for coffee ("Is it him?" "No!"). As a matter of fact it isn't anyone, I just don't feel like continuing the discussion. I shouldn't have mentioned Lewis in the first place, but after years of being single, there's part of me that takes pride in my newly coupled-up status, that finds reasons to insert the phrase "my boyfriend" into conversations with my friends, my clients, the lady at the corner Starbucks, and yes, even my mom.

This is a huge mistake, however, because three hours later my brother Jim is booked on a flight to visit me for the weekend.

Of course, the timing could be entirely coincidental. Jim is actually coming to New York to attend a conference—he works in real estate for a company in Topeka. He doesn't have to go to this particular conference, but he tells me that since his company will pay for his ticket—and since he's got a free place to stay—and since we haven't seen each other in a while—he figures he might as well. But I can't help but suspect there's another, unstated reason—which is that, having been unable to get sufficient details from me over the phone, my mother has put him up to it.

Nonetheless, I'm excited to see him. Jim's four years older, and we were close growing up, but ever since I moved away to go to college (he stayed close to home and went to Kansas State), our visits have been mostly limited to my twice-yearly trips back home, a week at Christmas and a week over the summer. He came to New York to see me once, right after Ben and I broke up, and helped me move some of my stuff into Mel and Nat's place . . . but I spent most of that visit prostrate on the floor, crying, so I wasn't really able to show him around. This time I'm looking forward to taking him out, showing him the sights—and the bars—and having a great time.

But somehow, as the visit approaches, I find reasons not to mention it to Lewis. He asks me if I want to go to the Philharmonic Friday and I tell him I can't, I've got plans with friends; he asks if I want to go to the movies Saturday and I tell him Linda wants me to work. He accepts my excuses with equanimity, which makes me feel guilty; apparently his belief in my inherent good nature is so strong that he doesn't even suspect that I would try to deceive him. (And it's not that I'm trying to *deceive* him, exactly . . . I'm just not ready to introduce him to my family yet. After all, we've only just started dating—at least officially—and I haven't entirely made my peace with our fledgling romance. And if something should happen and they should somehow find out who he really was . . . well, I don't even want to think about that.)

So keeping Lewis away from Jim is easy . . . keeping Jim away from Lewis, however, is another story. The airport shuttle drops him off outside my building Thursday evening. I come down to the lobby to meet him, and after we exchange greetings and hugs, he doesn't even wait until we're in the elevator to ask: "So where's your new boyfriend?"

"Oh. He's, uh—he's working late tonight."

"Oh, that's too bad."

"Yeah, he's, uh—he's really busy all weekend, actually. So you might not get a chance to meet him."

"He couldn't take an hour off to come have lunch, or something?"

"Um. No, I—don't think so. His job's, uh—it's pretty important."

"What did you say the company's called that he works for again?" Jim asks.

"Um. You know? I forget." Jim gives me a quizzical look. "It's one of those big multinational companies."

"Huh," Jim says.

After we drop off Jim's suitcase in the living room—he'll be sleeping on the couch—we decide to head out to a tapas restaurant called Lola's, on Third Avenue, to get some Spanish food. Mel's working late, but Nat's in her room performing some complicated beauty ritual involving her face, an avocado, a jar of honey, and a cucumber, so I invite her to come with us. She's been instructed—under pain of death—not to say the words "Satan" and "Lucy's boyfriend" in the same sentence, so I'm not worried she'll give away my secret. As it turns out, though, that's not what I need to be worried about.

Jim and Nat have met before, when Jim came to New York to help me move out of Ben's apartment. At the time, though, Jim was still dating Stephanie, his college girlfriend. Stephanie was a petite blonde with the face of an angel and the personality of a total psychopath. She and Jim met their junior year at Kansas State, then lived together for six years after graduation in Topeka. Jim was working for the real estate firm where he's still employed, and Stephanie was an aide at a nursing home, though her full-time job seemed to be pestering Jim about when they were going to get married.

My mother—and I, from a distance—had serious reservations about whether such a marriage would be a good idea, but Jim was seriously in love with Stephanie, and was only waiting until he could save up enough to get her the ring she "deserved" (two-carat, princess-cut, in a platinum setting.) Three months after he slipped it into her wine glass at the best Italian restaurant in Topeka, Stephanie decided she didn't want to get married after all, so she cheated on him with one of his friends, moved out, and sold the ring on eBay. This was two years ago, and Jim hasn't entirely gotten over her yet. Once he falls for a girl, he's totally devoted, as evidenced by the fact that last time he was here he barely looked twice at Natalie. But this time it's another story.

I decide not to change for dinner and just to wear the clothes I wore to work—a black skirt and a green v-neck sweater, with sensible low heels. Jim is still in the jeans and button-down he wore on the plane. But Nat, who believes in looking good whenever she leaves the house (not that she usually has to try very hard), emerges in a bright blue BCBG silk dress with brown leather boots and a brown leather jacket. When she comes into the living room with a perky "Okay! I'm ready!" I can tell from the look on Jim's face that he's impressed.

At dinner, we share ham and potato croquettes, a goat cheese torta, a spinach salad and cold poached shrimp, along with a bottle of rioja. Then, after the bottle is empty, Nat decides she wants to try one of the imported grappas on the menu as an after-dinner drink. "Let's each get one!" she suggests, but I beg off, saying I have to work tomorrow. She gives Jim a flirtatious glance. "How about you?" she says.

"Well . . . I don't have to be at the conference till eleven," he says with a shrug and a sheepish smile.

So they order two shots of grappa and drink them, and then they order two more, after which Natalie drags me into the bathroom and announces that my brother is "kind of cute." And it's true, Jim's a good-looking guy, about six-two, with blond hair, blue eyes, and an open, honest face. "Would it be totally weird if I hooked up with him?" Nat asks me.

"Um."

"It would, wouldn't it," she says. "Okay. I won't hook up with him." She takes her coral-colored lipstick out of her black fringed clutch and reapplies it carefully in the mirror. "I definitely won't hook up with him."

"So I'm going dancing tonight," she announces as soon as we sit back down at the table. "Who's in?"

"That sounds like fun," Jim says, looking at me hopefully.

"I can't," I tell them. "Linda wants me in early—our clients are coming into town for a meeting tomorrow."

"Well," Jim says. "I could still go. If you didn't mind me tagging along."

"Not at all," Natalie says, and gives him a dazzling smile.

"Is that okay with you, Luce?" Jim asks.

"Sure," I tell him. "Fine."

I want to somehow warn Jim about Natalie. Jim, after all, is a genuinely good guy, and Nat has been nothing but tragedy for any man she's ever gotten involved with. But I can't think of a way to pull him aside and talk to him without it seeming odd. And I doubt it would do much good—given the way he's watching Nat toss her hair and run her tongue provocatively along the rim of her glass, he's already a lost cause.

Besides, given the way I've been spending my own time lately, I'm hardly in a position to be offering anyone else romantic advice. So before I know it, we're hugging goodbye at the door, and I'm walking towards home while Jim and Nat are hailing a cab to go downtown to Avenue, where there's a party hosted by some girls Nat knows from modeling.

When I get up at seven a.m. for work the next morning, the couch is empty. I laid out a blanket and a couple of pillows before I went to bed the night before, but the blanket is unwrinkled and the pillows are just as I left them. Jim's shoes, however, are on the floor on the front hall carpet . . . and so are his pants. This is not a good sign.

Jim's on the couch when I come home after work, though . . . and curled up next to him, holding his hand, is Natalie. They're watching *Sleepless in Seattle*, Jim's other hand resting on Nat's leggings-clad knee, a smile on his face that reminds me of the way he used to look on his birthday when we were kids. If I didn't know Nat so well, I would think it was adorable.

"Hey, Luce!" they chorus in tandem when I come through the door.

"Um. Hi, guys. Nat, can I talk to you for a second?"

She disentangles herself from Jim, giving him a quick peck on the lips, and I practically drag her into my closet and shut the door behind her. "What's up?" she says cheerfully.

"I thought you weren't going to hook up with my brother."

She giggles. "Yeah. Oops."

"Oops?"

"What's wrong?" she says. "I mean, he's single, right?"

"Yeah, he's single, but Nat, he's my brother."

"Yeah, he's your brother, and I'm your best friend," she says, sounding genuinely confused. "You should be happy for us."

"You're my best friend," I tell her, "but you're not very—"

"What?"

I try to think of a way to put this without hurting her feelings. "You're not always very nice to guys." She looks offended and starts to open her mouth, and I put up a hand to stop her. "I mean you are for a little while, until you get tired of them . . . and then you move on. And that's fine—honestly, most of the guys you're with probably don't deserve any better. But . . . Jim does."

Natalie looks thoughtful, drawing her perfect brows together in silent contemplation, and for a moment I'm hopeful that maybe I've gotten through to her. "He's really sweet," she says finally.

"Yeah. He is."

"But Luce, I mean, he doesn't even live here. It's not like it could go anywhere even if either of us wanted it to. I think you're worrying too much. He and I both know we're just having fun."

I'm not convinced Jim knows this, but I'm also not sure how to tell him. After all, he's my older brother—he's the one who's supposed to be giving *me* advice. And besides, maybe Nat's right. Jim lives in Topeka, and Nat lives in New York City. Maybe he just sees this as a fling, the same way she does. Maybe I'm worrying too much and I just need to let the two of them have fun.

So that night, I decide that's what I'm going to do. Mel's staying over at Brandon's, so the three of us order pizza and then go out to a dive bar called McFly's on Second Avenue. It's the sort of place where your heels stick to the floor, should you be unwise enough to go in wearing heels—Nat and I have been there a few times, so we've learned to stick to flats. I've borrowed a pair of hers for the night . . . cute silver shoes with Lucite buckles, which I've paired with jeans and a white tank top. Nat's wearing a black blazer, a silver sequined tank, leggings, and slouchy black suede boots. She looks fantastic, of course, and Jim hardly takes his eyes off her.

McFly's has a great jukebox, and soon Nat and Jim are dancing to Michael Jackson, leaving me free to sneak outside, smoke a cigarette bummed from the bouncer, and call Lewis. I tell him I miss him, and he tells me to come over later. I tell him I will if I can get away.

Nat and Jim and I walk back from the bar together sometime after midnight, the two of them holding hands and belting out "Black or White." They quickly disappear into Nat's bedroom, and I go back outside and take a cab down to Lewis' place, where we spend a couple of blissful hours in his bed . . . and on his couch . . . and on his kitchen counter. I want to stay over, but I know if I'm not home in the morning Jim will start asking questions again, so I make up an excuse about having to go in to the office early the next morning and catch a cab back home.

The next day, Nat has a photo shoot, and Jim tells me he wants to take me out to lunch for some brother-sister time. I'm afraid this means some questions-about-Lewis time, but it's worse than that. We walk up to the Cosi at Forty-Third Street and order sandwiches—mozzarella and tomato for me, turkey, bacon and arugula for Jim. And as soon as we're comfortably settled into a booth, Jim announces that he's thinking about moving to New York City.

"*What?*"

"Wouldn't that be great?" he says. "We could hang out all the time."

"I mean—yeah, it'd be great, but—since when? Why?"

"I . . . I think I'm falling in love with Natalie," Jim says.

Oh, no. "In *love?* Jim, you just met her two days ago."

"That's not true," he says. "I met her a few years ago, when I came out to help you move."

"Yeah, okay, but you were with Stephanie then. You didn't

even talk to Nat."

"I know," he says. "But I could tell she had a beautiful soul."

*You could tell she had a beautiful ass,* I want to tell him. "Jim. Um. If you're moving here because of Nat . . . that isn't a good idea."

"I know it seems impulsive," he says, "but I've never connected with anybody this way. She's just . . . I don't know. She's perfect. But it's not just because of her. I've been doing tons of networking at the conference—I think I could get a job here, and there's a lot more opportunity to move up than there is in Topeka. And you're here. I'd get to spend more time with my sis." He reaches out and gives my forearm an affectionate squeeze.

"Yeah. I know. I just—I'm not—I'm not sure things with you and Nat are going to work out. She's a great friend, but she's . . . she's not a very good girlfriend—if she's ever actually been anyone's girlfriend—which I'm pretty sure she hasn't."

Jim's face turns cold and he's quiet for a moment. "How come I haven't gotten to meet your boyfriend?" he asks finally. "Where's he been?"

"I told you," I say. "He's been busy with work."

"Yeah, well, if he's so busy with work that he can't spare a half hour to come and meet your brother, then I'm not sure things with you and him are going to work out either."

"I don't know if they are or not," I tell him. "But that's not what we're talking about."

"You worry about your love life, and I'll worry about mine, okay?" Jim says. He pushes back his chair and stands, though we're not even done with our sandwiches. "You ready to go?"

Silently, I wrap up the other half of my tomato and mozzarella baguette and pick up my diet Coke. We walk back to the apartment mostly in silence—I try to engage Jim by asking him questions about how Mom and Dad are doing, but he just gives me one word answers. "Look, I'll stay out of your business," I tell him finally, as we're waiting for the elevator in my lobby. "I was just trying to help."

"I don't need your help," he says.

"I know. I'm sorry."

Jim could never stay mad at me for long, not even the time I accidentally knocked a whole can of paint over on his science fair project—an elaborate ant farm he'd been working on for days. "It's okay," he says. "Hey, you want to hear a funny story about the baby?"

"The baby" is what Jim calls Mom's tiny toy poodle, Coco. He likes to joke that Coco is Mom's replacement for me, since she got the dog as soon as I went away to school. Coco is barely a foot tall, even standing on her hind legs, but apparently she somehow managed to get up on the kitchen counter and eat her way through an entire pan of brownies that were cooling there . . . then vomit all over the expensive Turkish carpet in the front hall.

"They're lucky she didn't die!" I tell him. "Chocolate is really poisonous for dogs."

"I know," he says, "and she literally ate her body weight in brownies. Got her little snout up in that pan and licked it clean."

I chuckle, picturing Coco's tiny white furry snout covered in brownie crumbs. "I think I'm going to head to the gym," I tell him. "You want to come with? I've got guest passes."

"Sure," he says.

"Hey, Jim?" I ask as I'm heading into the closet to change. "Have you told Natalie anything about how you're thinking about moving to New York?"

"Not yet," he says. "I think I will tonight."

I want to tell him not to, but I don't want to start another fight. "Okay."

"Why?" he says.

"No reason."

# — 20 —

THAT NIGHT, JIM, Nat, Mel and I go to a Mexican place near Union Square called La Rosarita. Mel, who's hardly been around all week, is taken aback when Jim and Nat start making out in the cab on the way to the restaurant. Once we get there, I pull her into the bathroom with me, telling Jim and Nat that I need her to help me fix my eye makeup.

In the bright light of the ladies' room, Mel produces a tiny bottle of black liquid liner from her purse and begins rimming my eyes with it while I explain the situation. She seems distracted, and a couple of times she asks me to repeat what I just said, but eventually I make it through the story of the past two nights. "That doesn't sound good," she says when I've finished.

"No, and it gets even worse," I tell her. "Jim wants to move to New York, and he's going to tell her so. Tonight."

Mel shakes her head.

"I don't know what she'll do," I continue as Mel re-caps the liner and slips it into her purse. "But I know what she *won't* do, which is tell him she wants to be in a committed relationship. I'm just hoping she doesn't freak out and decide to show him he shouldn't move here by making out with somebody else in front of him, or something."

I look over at Mel. She's staring vaguely at her reflection in one of the tooled silver Mexican mirrors above the sinks. "Mel? You don't think she'll do anything like that . . . do you?"

"Huh?" Mel says.

"Are you okay? You seem really out of it."

"Yeah," she says. "I'm—I've just been—yeah. I'm fine. It's just been a really busy week." She pulls herself together, turning away from the mirror, smiling at me, and linking her arm through mine. "Let's go start drinking, 'kay?"

When we sit down at the table, there's a round of margaritas on it, and Natalie, with a frozen smile on her face, is draining hers. She puts down her empty glass and signals to the waiter for another.

"Make it two," Jim calls over to the waiter. "We've got a lot to celebrate tonight." He smiles at Mel and me. "Just told Nat the good news."

"That you're—?"

"Yup," he says. "That I'm moving. Soon as I can get my place rented out back home."

I take a giant gulp of my margarita. From the corner of my eye, I see that Mel is doing the same thing. The waiter brings over a tray with two more margaritas for Jim and Nat on it.

"Well, um . . . cheers!" I say, raising my glass to the table.

"Cheers!" they chorus in return, Mel and Nat half-heartedly, though Jim's voice is hearty enough to make up for it.

After we've had some guacamole and tacos and flautas, and talked about work and the weather and the upcoming election and how the Kansas State football team is doing and everything *but* Jim's move, Jim says: "So where are we heading after this?"

"I'm actually going to go see this band play in the East Village," Nat says. "I'm friends with the drummer. But you guys don't have to come."

"I'll come," Jim says quickly.

"No, you should—you should spend some time with Lucy," Nat says.

"Lucy'll come too. Won't she?" he asks, turning to me.

"Lucy, um—Lucy doesn't like this band very much," Nat says. I have no idea what band she's talking about, of course.

"Come on, Luce," Jim says. "I'll buy you a beer."

Natalie gives me a pleading look—but I'm not letting her off the hook so easily. She got herself into this situation, and she'll have to get herself out of it. "Sure," I say. "I'll come."

"Great!" Jim says, and the next thing I know, the four of us are in a cab heading towards the East Village. The cab lets us off in front of a plain black door on First Avenue. There's no sign on the door, but Nat punches in a key code and we go down a flight of stairs to a small, dark basement, covered with graffiti, where a crowd of hipsters press against each other while trying to make their way up to the bar. In the front of the room is a stage where a band is tuning up.

"I'll go get us drinks," Jim says, and as he attempts to fight his way through the crowd, I see Nat blowing a kiss to the pale, tattooed, lank-haired drummer. He blows her one back. I look at Mel, trying to catch her eye, but she's staring off into space again.

When Jim returns with our drinks, the band has started playing, if "playing" is the word. The lead singer is howling like a wounded dog, the guitarist is playing something that bears no resemblance to harmony, and the drummer seems to be striking his drums completely at random. But Nat has migrated up to the front of the crowd, next to the stage, and started dancing enthusiastically. Jim hands off two of the drinks—a beer for me, and a vodka soda for Mel—and then starts pushing his way between the hipsters to get to her.

But by the time he's at the front of the room, she's already got a beer in each hand . . . two other guys have bought them for her. Jim holds up the beer he's bought and she shrugs and laughs, tossing her hair. He tries to take her by the waist and dance with her, but Nat jumps up onstage and starts dancing there instead. The drummer abandons his drums entirely, stands up, and starts grinding with her as the crowd cheers, and I see Jim chugging first his beer, then the one he bought for Nat as he watches them.

I tap Mel on the arm and yell: "I'll be right back!" and she nods vaguely. I push my way in between hips, shoulders, elbows until I get to the front of the room and grab Jim's shoulder. "Hey!" I yell at him over the noise of the band.

"What is she doing?" Jim yells back, gesturing at Nat dancing onstage.

"She's just . . . being Natalie," I tell him. "Do you want to go? Let's go."

"Only if she comes with us!" he yells.

I try to catch Nat's eye, but she's wholly absorbed in grinding her ass against the drummer's crotch. I reach up and grab her foot. She looks down.

"Hey! Nat! Let's go!"

"I don't want to go!" she yells. "I'm having fun!"

"Then I don't want to go either," Jim tells me.

"Come on, Jim. It's only going to get worse!" But he doesn't hear me. Which doesn't much matter, because Nat, still dancing, spins around so she's face to face with the drummer, and a moment later his tongue is halfway down her throat. The crowd cheers even louder as they make out, and Jim slams his fist down on the bar.

"Damn it, Luce! What is she—why is she—"

I can't stand to see the hurt in his eyes. "Come on," I say firmly, grabbing his arm this time. "We're going to go."

# – 21 –

JIM HAS TO LEAVE for the airport early the next morning, and I get up to make him coffee and see him off. I don't know if Natalie ever came home, but if she did, she certainly doesn't emerge from her room to say goodbye. Which is just as well, because if she did I'd probably throw my coffee in her face.

I know Jim was up late, because I heard the TV playing in the living room from inside my closet the night before. "Did you get any sleep?" I ask him.

"No," he says, rubbing his eyes. "Not really." He's stuffing his clothes into his duffel bag.

"Well. I'm—I'm sorry you didn't have a good time."

"Not your fault," he says, and gives my shoulder a squeeze. "It was great to see you."

"Yeah," I tell him. "You too." And it was. I'd forgotten how nice it was having him around. For a moment I let myself think about what it would be like if things were different . . . if Natalie weren't such a tease . . . if Jim actually moved to the city and the two of them actually dated. It would be so much fun.

"And I still want to meet this mysterious boyfriend of yours," Jim says.

"Yeah. Well, if we . . . if it works out, I'm sure you will eventually."

Just then the intercom buzzes. "Ms. O'Neill? Your cab is here," the doorman says, and Jim enfolds me in a hug.

"Good luck with everything," he says.

"Yeah. You too. Are you—are you okay?"

Jim gives me a smile and a shrug, and then heads out the door.

After he leaves, I want to go back to bed, but I've had coffee, and I'm wired. I think about calling Lewis to see if he wants to have brunch, but it's only eight a.m. and I'm not sure he'll be up yet. I turn on the TV and watch old reruns of Rachael Ray for an hour while painting my nails red. Just as I've finished my right hand and am about to start on my left, Nat breezes through the door, still dressed in the skintight jeans, black tank top, brown leather jacket and boots she was wearing last night.

"Hey, Luce!" she says cheerfully. I say nothing. "You guys just, like, disappeared last night," she continues. "Where'd you go?"

I look up. "Home," I tell her, and look back down at my nails.

"Oh. How come?" she asks.

It takes a Herculean effort, but once again I say nothing.

"I mean, I thought we were all having fun," Nat says.

And now it's impossible—I can't keep quiet any longer. "You thought Jim was having fun?" I ask her.

"Well, maybe not him," she says. "But all us girls."

"He's not just a guy, Nat!" I tell her. "He's my brother!"

"Yeah, I know," she says innocently.

"And even if he weren't . . . he's a really good person and he doesn't deserve to have you treat him like that. I mean you can't just—you can't just go around treating people like shit and get away with it forever!"

"I didn't treat him like shit," she says. "We had some fun, and then I had some fun with someone else."

"You didn't just have some fun, Nat. He was falling in love with you."

"Okay," she says, "maybe, but it's not like that's my fault."

"It is, though, because you do this all the time! You make men fall in love with you, and then you stomp all over their hearts, and you enjoy it! And I think it's just because you're scared . . . maybe it's because your dad died, I don't know, but you're too scared to let yourself get close to anybody!"

I've thought this before, but I've never said it aloud. In every friendship there are probably certain things that are true but should never be spoken. Nat goes white.

"I don't know how you could say something like that," she

says in a small, tight voice. "You're just jealous because I can get any guy I want, and the only guy who's been interested in you in the last four years is Satan."

She picks up her bag, which she's thrown down on the kitchen counter, and leaves the apartment, slamming the door behind her.

# – 22 –

I DON'T KNOW where Nat's gone or when she'll come back, but I certainly don't feel like seeing her when she does, so I take a shower and pack some clothes into a bag for work tomorrow, planning to stay overnight at Lewis' place. Mel's in the kitchen when I come out of the shower, drinking the remaining cup of coffee from the pot I made for Jim. I tell her about what just happened.

"Mmmm," she says distractedly when I've finished the story.

"So what do you think? I mean I probably shouldn't have said that. But I think I had a right to say it—didn't I?" Mel is twirling a piece of her blonde hair and staring out the window at the skyscrapers outside. The sky is gray and a slow drizzle is falling. She doesn't say anything. "Mel? Are you okay?"

"Huh?" she says.

"You've been totally out of it every time I've seen you all—well, I *haven't* seen you all week, until last night, and then last night and this morning you've been totally out of it. Is there something going on?"

"No, I'm fine," she says. "I'm just tired. Sorry."

"Cause you know, if something was wrong, you could tell me . . ." I press her.

"Yeah, I know," she says. She takes the last sip of her coffee, puts the cup in the dishwasher, and twists her hair up in a businesslike knot with the hair tie around her wrist. "What are you up to today?" she asks me with a bright smile. "Heading down to see Lewis?"

"Yeah . . . what about you?"

"I think I'm going to go for a long run," she says. "Down along the river."

"Do you think maybe you're training too hard?" I ask her. "I mean, if you're tired all the time . . . ?"

"Training too hard? No such thing," she says cheerfully, and heads into her room to change into her running gear.

I'm still concerned about her, but I'm not sure what I can do about it, since she's obviously not in a mood to confide. And besides, it wasn't like she was particularly concerned about *me* . . . which you'd think she would be, given that Nat and I are her two best friends—and roommates—and I'm not sure when we'll be back on speaking terms.

Feeling disappointed in both my friends, I trudge through the drizzle to catch the subway downtown to Lewis' place. Maybe some steamy sex will cheer me up. Lewis and I have recently begun using handcuffs, and it's been a revelation. "Sometimes it's good to be a little bit bad," he'd said with a wicked smile the night he first produced them from his dresser drawer.

And it does cheer me up . . . for a while. After I spend a couple of hours handcuffed to his headboard, Lewis suggests venturing out into the rain for dinner. There's a wood-fired pizza place nearby that we've been to a couple of times, and on this cold, rainy night, pizza sounds perfect. We walk down the street together, arm in arm, sharing a single umbrella, to the restaurant.

But once we're there, waiting for our pizza with buffalo mozzarella, sausage, and black olives to appear, I find myself uncharacteristically quiet. Lewis is a great listener, and I'm usually able to talk to him about whatever's on my mind . . . but explaining what's on my mind tonight would mean explaining that my brother was in town all weekend, which would mean explaining that I'd been lying to Lewis about being at work instead of introducing the two of them. Which is not an explanation I'm willing to get into just yet.

Lewis asks me a couple of times what's wrong, since I'm staring into my diet Coke instead of talking. I tell him nothing, I'm just tired from work . . . hearing an echo of Mel telling me the same thing in the kitchen that morning. He looks at me skeptically, but doesn't question my explanation.

"You know," he says instead, "Linda should really pay you more, given that you work as hard as you do. What do you make—fifty?" I hesitate. "Less?"

"Forty-five," I admit. It sounds so paltry. Lewis can make three times what I earn in a year in a single weekend.

"And you work weekends," he says, "a lot of weekends—right?" I hadn't actually worked this weekend, but I do work a lot of weekends. I nod. "When was the last time you got a raise?" he asks.

"Um . . ." I'm trying to remember if I've ever gotten a raise. "Oh! After my first year. I started at forty."

"And you haven't gotten one since?"

"Linda doesn't make a lot either. It's a new company and we're trying to grow, but—"

"But that's no excuse for underpaying you," he interrupts me. "I wasn't kidding when I said I could get you a job at one of the bigger firms."

My hand has been resting on his on top of the table, but now I pull it back and push back my chair. "I already told you I don't want to steal Linda's client!—and you said you weren't going to—"

"Lucy! Relax. I'm not trying to talk you into doing something bad. I'm trying to talk you into doing something good. I know you don't want to steal the client . . . I just think you should ask for a raise."

"Oh."

He reaches out and takes my hand again. "You're so sweet, and that's one of the things I like so much about you." He smiles, and I feel myself melting. "But sometimes that means you don't stand up for what you really deserve."

I consider this, stirring the ice in my diet Coke and wondering if he's right. I come in whenever Linda calls me, even on Sunday mornings—and I know I'm good at my job. "I'll think about it," I tell him.

"Good," he says. "Oh, by the way, speaking of work—I'm going to have to go out of town next week for a little while."

"Out of town where?" I ask him. "Back to Vegas?"

"No, to Hell actually," he says. "There are some administrative things I have to attend to."

"What kind of . . . administrative things?" I ask him, and then realize I probably don't want to know. Is "administrative things" code for torturing sinners?

As he often does, Lewis responds based on the look on my face. "I'm not actually in charge of administering punishments," he says. "That's not what I mean."

"Who's in charge of that, then?"

"Well, there are hordes of demons who are responsible for carrying them out."

"Hordes of demons," just doesn't seem like a phrase that ought to be uttered in a cozy brick oven pizzeria. "But you decide what they are?"

"No, actually," he says, "they're cosmically prescribed. The universe operates according to certain laws . . . you throw an apple, it comes down again . . . you commit murder, you spend eternity boiling in a river of blood."

"Wow."

Lewis starts to chuckle, and I look at him, confused. I fail to see what's so funny about boiling in a river of blood. "No, no, no," he says. "I'm not laughing at that. It's just funny because sometimes the punishments change . . . evolve . . . as the world changes."

"Okay . . ."

"Like, for example, if you commit adultery . . . you have an affair while you're married . . . the punishment used to be that you'd spend eternity being blown around a dreary plain by hurricane winds."

"Used to be? What is it now?"

"Now you have to watch a sex tape—of the person you loved most in the world, whether it's your spouse, or your lover—with somebody else. Over and over. Forever."

I laugh in spite of myself. "How do you get the sex tapes? Are they real?"

"Yeah, there are some demons that are pretty tiny . . . they can climb through windows, hide behind pillows, that sort of thing. So we give them little cameras, and . . ."

"Wow." As always, when Lewis talks about his work, I'm torn between wanting to know everything, and wanting him to stop talking about it so I can just pretend he's a normal guy, a guy who's not sending tiny demons through people's windows with cameras. "So what are the administrative affairs you have to attend to?"

"Basically just check up on things, make sure everything's running the way it's supposed to," he says. "Beelzebub and Astaroth pretty much keep things going, but I do have to check in from time to time. I usually spend a week down there each month . . . but I haven't been down in almost two months . . . not since I met you."

"So . . . when are you leaving?"

"Tomorrow," he says.

"And how long are you going to be gone?"

"Just a few days," he says. "I should be back Thursday or Friday."

The prospect of a few days without Lewis—especially now that Nat is (at least temporarily) dead to me, and Mel is off in her own world—stretches in front of me like a desert. "That's a long time."

Lewis smiles. "You going to miss me?"

I look down and take a giant bite of sausage and mozzarella, not wanting to admit how much. With a mouth full of pizza, all I can do is nod.

"I'm going to miss you too," he says.

"How do you get there?" I ask him. "To Hell, I mean."

"There are portals all over the world," he says. "Doors that lead down, if you know where they are. Here in New York, the portal happens to be in the subway."

I laugh. "That's about right."

"Yeah," he says, "it's near the RW train platform at Canal Street. That station's always been unusually warm, and no one knows why . . . the MTA workers are always talking about it."

"So you just . . ."

"You walk down the tracks," he says, "until you get to the door, which is a little ways down the tunnel, and then you open it. I usually try to go in the middle of the night, when there's nobody there. Otherwise you get some odd looks when you climb down off the subway platform."

"But what if somebody else were to open the door—would they end up in Hell accidentally?"

"It's very unlikely. It's not just an ordinary door . . . it's enchanted. You can look straight at it and not even know it's there, unless you happen to be looking for it. And nobody—except for me—ever goes looking for it."

LEWIS OFFERS to leave me his keys and let me stay at his place while he's away, but honestly, the thought of being in the apartment without him kind of gives me the creeps. As long as he and I are together, it doesn't much matter where we are, but the apartment's so big and empty and somehow impersonal that without him it would just feel strange.

And then there's the closet full of fire, which is merrily burning away again after the fire department's intercession. Lewis has told me he likes to go and sit in there and think . . . it reminds him of home. He's assured me that he has the power to control fire, and he won't let it escape, but I hate to think what might happen if he weren't home and the fire somehow managed to melt the seals around the closet door again.

So at five a.m. the next morning, I share a cab with him uptown. We stop first at the Canal Street station, where he gets out and kisses me goodbye, then hands the cabbie a twenty and tells him to continue on to my place. Watching him walk down the steps to the subway, then turn around, smile, and blow me a kiss, I have a feeling it's going to be a very long few days.

When I get back to my apartment it's only five-thirty, but I figure that since I'm up I might as well make some coffee and go into the office early. Nat and Mel both have their doors closed. Nat's probably out having sex on a pool table somewhere, and Mel must still be sleeping. This will probably be the first time

I've *ever* left for work before Mel did.

As I'm going down the hall to the shower, though, I'm halted by muffled sounds coming from behind Mel's door. If it weren't for the fact that I'd never seen her cry—not even in college, when she found out her first serious boyfriend had been cheating on her with the president—the male president—of the student council, I'd think she was crying. I wrap my bright pink towel more securely around my chest and knock on the door. "Mel? Are you okay?"

A moment later, the door opens. Mel's looking perfectly composed in her cream-colored cashmere bathrobe, her blonde hair loose around her face. "Luce? What are you doing up so early?"

"I was at Lewis's. Is everything all right? I thought—I thought I heard crying."

Mel shakes her head. Her eyes are dry, and not at all red. "I was playing my music . . . really softly."

"Maybe that's what I heard," I tell her. Although it seems odd that she would have turned the music off before she opened the door. "Sorry. Do you need the bathroom?—you mind if I use the shower?"

"Go ahead," she says, and is about to shut the door again when I stop her.

"Hey. You haven't—you haven't talked to Nat, have you?"

"I haven't seen her," Mel says. "I've been working late, and then she's been out for the night by the time I've gotten home."

"So what do you think I should do?" I ask her. "I mean, I'm still mad about the Jim thing—but she's my best friend—"

"Look, Luce," Mel says. "I've got a lot on my mind right now, with work and . . . and everything, and I really don't have time to worry about you and Natalie fighting. I'm sorry."

And with that, she shuts the door in my face, leaving me standing, stunned, in the hallway.

# – 23 –

LUCKILY, IT'S A BUSY day at work, so I don't have too much time to spend moping about the fact that not only is my boyfriend out of town, but I'm also now somehow fighting with *both* of my best friends. Kruger has decided to come out with a line of small kitchen appliances—toasters, blenders, and so on—and so we're pitching them to every media outlet on our lists. We work straight through lunch, ordering in salads from a restaurant around the corner, and we're in the office until eight p.m . . . and in between phone calls to reporters, I find myself thinking about what Lewis said. I work long hours for a salary that's barely enough to live on, at least in Manhattan. Maybe I really should ask for a raise. It couldn't hurt. The worst Linda could do is say no.

So the next morning, I screw up my courage and go into the inner office to talk to her about it. After I make my case—I work hard, I've been there for four years, the cost of living has gone up—Linda looks down at her desk and buries her head in her hands. *Oh, no. I shouldn't have asked.* Then she looks up. "Well," she says, "you know you're invaluable and I don't want to lose you. Money is tight, but let me think about it and see what I can do."

Later that afternoon, she comes out and tells me she can bump me up to fifty-two thousand, starting in January. It's not a lot, but it's a lot more than I was making, and I'm elated. I want to call Lewis and tell him all about it, but cell phones and email aren't able to bridge the gap between the underworld and this one, and he's told me he'll be incommunicado for the week.

As I'm walking home after work, though, I check my phone and see that I have a message from an unfamiliar number. Maybe Lewis has figured out some way to call me after all? I press 1 to listen to my voicemail . . . and my heart skips a beat, as an entirely different male voice comes through the phone.

"Hi. Lucy. It's, uh—it's Ben. I'm really sorry to call you, I just—" His voice catches. "I just don't know what else to do. I, uh—I lost my job. Lerner Locke, they're, uh—they're downsizing—they're not doing very well—and I, uh—I can't make my rent, so I ended up getting evicted from my apartment. And Kelly and I—with all the stress, we, uh—we broke up. And now I don't have anywhere to go, and I'm wondering if there's any chance I could possibly crash with you for a little while. Just a couple of days. I'm so sorry to ask you this, I just—I honestly don't have anywhere else to turn. Most of my friends were work friends, or her friends, and now . . . well, I remember you told me once that if I ever needed anything . . . and I do. So if you could call me back. Please."

I almost drop my phone to the sidewalk. Fortunately, I manage to catch it on its way down and return it to its place in the front pocket of my leather tote bag. I've stopped stock still in the middle of the sidewalk on Thirty-Fourth Street to listen to the voicemail, and people are circling around me . . . or bumping into me. I duck into the Starbucks on the corner, sit down at the front counter, then take out my phone and listen to the message again, thinking about what I should do.

I *had* told Ben that if he ever needed anything, he could come to me. This was after our breakup, when he'd revealed to me that he'd been sleeping with Kelly, his shapely blonde coworker, for the past three months, and was going to break up with me to be with her . . . and that as a result, I was going to have to move out of our apartment. It was as I was moving the last of my boxes, about to get in the cab that would take me over to Melissa and Natalie's place. I'd told him, through my tears, that I still loved him in spite of everything, and if he ever needed anything from me all he would have to do was ask. It makes me cringe now just thinking about it.

Ben and I have hardly talked since we split up. There was some talk of remaining friends, and we went out for coffee a couple of times, but for me it was painful and time-consuming . . . I had to borrow just the right outfit, apply enough makeup to look "done" but still "natural," obsess about whether I'd gained a couple of pounds since we broke up—only to spend an hour at Starbucks listening to Ben rattle on about how great his life was. As for Ben, I think he was more or less indifferent. After a few months, we just stopped calling each other . . . and beyond the occasional Google search (or, okay, the daily Google search—but only for the first few months!), I've had nothing to do with him since.

So what am I supposed to do now? I desperately wish I could call Natalie and Melissa, tell them to meet me at Vinoteca, and analyze the situation in depth over a bottle of wine. But that isn't going to happen. Instead I get in line, order a tall skim white chocolate mocha, and sit back down at the counter to analyze my options.

I know I'd be within my rights to blow him off completely. I certainly don't owe him anything, after the way he treated me. But, on the other hand, I'd said I'd help him out if he ever needed me to . . . and even though he didn't deserve it—then *or* now—it feels like I'd be going back on my word if I didn't follow through.

Besides, I have to admit that part of me likes the idea of Ben needing *me* for a change. My newly better-paid PR job might not be as glamorous as working at a top hedge fund, but at least it's secure. I might live in a closet, but at least I'm not getting evicted. My boyfriend might be the devil, but at least I have a boyfriend. I like the idea of showing Ben how well I'm doing without him.

So I pick up my phone, heart beating fast, find his number at the top of my missed call list, and press send. An hour later, there's a knock on my door. Ben, holding an enormous suitcase and wearing a sheepish smile, is standing outside in the hallway. I'm a little surprised that one suitcase is all he's got. He must have put the rest of his stuff into storage along with his furniture.

He looks good. He's let his curly blond hair, which he always kept cropped short, grow slightly longer, and he's in a grey Lacoste polo, jeans, and loafers. He looks casually sexy, like he belongs on a yacht, or in a cologne advertisement. His eyes widen when he sees me.

"Wow, Luce," he says. "You look fantastic. You cut your hair."

"Oh," I say casually, "yeah." I run a hand through my bouncy, highlighted waves. "Come in. You can put your suitcase in the living room—you'll be on the couch."

He drags his suitcase inside and sits down, stretching his legs out and admiring the view from the living room window. "This is a nice place," he says.

Usually when people say this kind of thing, I feel the need to make some kind of disparaging remark about how I live in the closet. But instead I just nod. "Yeah, we like it."

"Well, you're a lifesaver, Luce," he says. "Seriously. I don't even know how to thank you."

I look down at the rug, slightly embarrassed. "It's, uh—it's no problem."

"And you really do look great. I like that outfit."

I'm wearing Lewis' cashmere tracksuit. "Thanks," I tell him. "My, uh—my boyfriend got it for me."

"Oh," Ben says in a neutral voice. "You have a boyfriend?"

"Yeah."

"Wow, uh—since when? I mean, is it serious?"

"Just a couple of months," I tell him. "But it's going really well."

Am I imagining it, or is that a look of disappointment on Ben's face? He looks down at his loafers for a moment, then looks up and gives me a smile. "That's great," he says. "Couldn't have happened to a better girl. So tell me everything—how's life been going?"

And over the next couple of hours, I find myself telling Ben all about the problems I'm having with Natalie and Melissa. He knows them both well, of course, since we all went to school together. There's nobody else I've been able to talk to about the situation . . . and it's a relief just to have a sympathetic ear and tell somebody what I've been thinking about.

Ben, in turn, tells me all about his breakup with Kelly . . . which apparently took place shortly after he lost his job three months ago. Kelly had managed to keep hers, despite hard times at Lerner Locke, and hadn't looked favorably on Ben's failure to do the same. "She wanted to date a banker," he says, "not some guy who sits around in sweats on the couch."

"She should have wanted to date *you*," I tell him, "whatever your job was. If she didn't, she wasn't worth it."

"I know," he says, "you're right." He sighs. "So what about your boyfriend? What does he do?"

"Oh, he's, uh—he's a recruiter," I tell him.

"Pretty good money in that?" Ben asks.

"Um. Yeah. He does pretty well."

"I'm thinking this whole layoff thing might be a great excuse for a career change," Ben says. "Might want to get out of finance altogether. I've been thinking about HR actually—recruiting, headhunting, something like that. Maybe your boyfriend and I could chat sometime."

"Yeah. Um. He's out of town right now."

"Well, maybe when he gets back."

"Yeah. Maybe."

Just then Nat comes through the door. She's wearing heavy makeup, and looks as though she's been at a photo shoot. She stops dead in the entry hall, looking from me, to Ben, then back to me again. Then, without a word, she continues down the hallway to her bedroom.

Ben and I look at each other, then burst into stifled giggles. "Well, that was awkward," he says once we manage to get our laughter under control, and that sets us off all over again.

"Okay," I finally manage, as a few last giggles escape me. "I'd better go to bed—Linda wants me in early again tomorrow." I go over to my closet and grab a couple of pillows and a spare blanket that I keep at the bottom of my bed. "You okay?—you need anything else?"

"Nope," he says, "I'm all set. Thanks."

"Okay. There's a spare key hanging next to the fridge, so you can use that if you need to go out during the day. And I'll see you after work tomorrow, I guess."

"Hey," Ben says. "Give me a hug." I cross to him and we hug. A wave of nostalgia comes over me, feeling his body, so familiar and yet so strange, in my arms again. I let go quickly. "It's really great to hang out with you again."

"Yeah," I tell him, and I'm surprised to find that I genuinely mean it. "You too."

# – 24 –

THE NEXT NIGHT, Ben tells me he'll take me out to dinner as a thank you for letting him stay. I feel bad letting him spend money on me, seeing as he's unemployed, but he insists. We end up going to a nice place, a French bistro on Broadway called Peche, because we're walking by and he tells me he's always wanted to try it. It's rustic-looking and romantic, wood tables, candles, dim lights.

We order an appetizer (steak tartare, which scares me . . . but when I take a bite of the raw beef it's salty and clean-tasting) and two entrees—sole a la meunière for me, rib-eye for Ben. I tell him I'm way too full for dessert, but he orders a chocolate pot de crème and persuades me to take a bite, and I end up eating at least half of it. He reminds me that this is something I always used to do—when we were dating he made a policy of ordering two of whatever dessert he was having, because he knew I'd end up eating one of them. The bill has got to be astronomical, and I tell him I'll help him with it when the check comes—especially since he's unemployed now—but he says it's the least he can do.

He tells me he spent the day looking for apartments online, and he's supposed to go see a couple of places tomorrow. When I get home from work the next day I ask him about it, but he says they were both awful—in one, a rat scurried across the living room floor just as the owner was pointing out the original prewar moldings, and in the other, what was touted as a kitchen turned out to actually be a microwave in the corner. "I'll keep looking tomorrow," he says. "I promise I'll find a place and be out of your hair soon."

Honestly, I'm kind of enjoying having him around. I'm not sure how Nat and Mel feel about it, but I've hardly seen them and Ben hasn't either . . . Nat's been out and about, and Mel's been at work all the time. Of course, I'm sure Lewis would have some questions if he got back into town and found my ex-boyfriend sleeping on my couch . . . but he wouldn't necessarily have to know, since I usually go to his place anyway.

And Ben is good company. He's eager to do me small favors to repay me for having a place to stay: he picks up my dry cleaning, goes to the store to get milk and cereal, calls Verizon to have someone come and figure out why our wireless service keeps flickering on and off (a task we've been meaning to get around to, but haven't, for the past few months). It's almost like having a very attentive live-in boyfriend, of the kind that he never was when he actually *was* my live-in boyfriend. And he's always a sympathetic ear if I want to talk.

Which is what ends up getting me into trouble.

It happens on Friday, the third night he's staying at my place. It's been a stressful day at work . . . Kruger's not happy with the press release we put together for their toaster, so I've spent all afternoon going back and forth with Amy Klein, their V.P. of New Product Development. She's new to the Kruger team and incredibly critical, and I've emailed her six drafts which she's sent back covered with comments, telling me to change certain phrases, then, once I've changed them, to change them back to what they were before. Finally, after four hours of this, I swallow my pride and go into Linda's office to appeal for her help.

"Maybe you could talk to her? I'm sorry, I just—I don't understand what I'm supposed to do."

"Just figure it out, Lucy, will you!" she snaps at me. "I've got a call with a reporter from *Glamour* in five minutes. I didn't give you a raise so I would have to deal with this!"

I blink back my tears and go back into the outer office. Apparently nobody in my life has time to deal with me at the moment. Mel, who's supposed to be my best friend, certainly doesn't . . . and Linda, for whom I put in fifty-plus-hour work weeks, obviously doesn't either.

And neither, apparently, does Lewis . . . he said he'd be

back Thursday or Friday, but it's Friday afternoon and I haven't heard anything from him yet. Of course, it's possible his administrative affairs ended up taking longer than he expected, but it seems like he could have found some way to be in touch and let me know. After all, if he's got armies of miniature demons climbing through people's windows, he could have sent one of them to climb through mine with a note telling me that he's thinking about me.

Unless he *isn't* thinking about me, of course. Unless he's realized he prefers being down in Hell and wants to stay there. Unless he's reconnected with one of his former lovers . . . Mata Hari . . . or Marilyn Monroe . . . now dead, of course, but still beautiful . . . still far more sexy and fascinating than a boring, ordinary PR girl who can't even get a press release right. By eight p.m., when I finally give up on the press release and go home for the evening, I still haven't heard anything, and I've managed to convince myself that Lewis has probably forgotten about me entirely.

I'm expecting Ben to be out and about, but when I trudge into the apartment, exhausted and dispirited—and also wet, since a slow, steady drizzle has started falling outside—he's sitting on the couch. On the coffee table in front of him is a bottle of merlot and two plates heaping with Indian takeout. He's remembered that I like paneer tikka masala and garlic naan.

"You look stressed," he says. "Come sit down and tell me all about it."

And I do . . . over the bottle of merlot, and then over glasses of Frangelico, a hazelnut-flavored liqueur for which Ben has always had an inexplicable affection. He's brought a half-full bottle from his old apartment over in his suitcase. I usually think Frangelico tastes like cough syrup—hazelnut-flavored cough syrup—but after a couple of glasses of wine it's surprisingly tolerable.

By the time we break out the Frangelico, Ben has resurrected a game we used to play in college. His parents lived in Middlebury, Vermont, and I used to make the five-hour drive with him to visit them at least three or four weekends a year. On the long car rides we'd play a game we made up called "Top Five." One of us would name a category—"Top Five Love Songs," or "Top Five Museums," and the other would answer, and then turn it back around.

"Top five worst days at work," Ben says now, while pouring Frangelico into Mel's Columbia shot glasses.

I sigh dramatically. "The day I got hired." We both break into giggles.

"No, seriously," he says.

I think about it. "Today. And the day I went in even though I had strep. And the day I was eating lunch at my desk and spilled half a bottle of Italian dressing all over my computer. Linda was *not* happy about that."

"Did it recover?"

"No, she had to buy me a new one. And I lost a bunch of pretty important files. But really . . ." I try to think of other terrible days in the office, but nothing in particular comes to mind. "That's pretty much it. It isn't the perfect job . . . and I know I complain a lot . . . but I'm pretty happy."

"Cheers to that," Ben says, and we clink our glasses together and drink.

"What about you?" I ask him.

"Well," he says, "the day I got laid off."

"Yeah."

"But also every day for a long time before that. I loved Lerner Locke at first, but honestly, it had been really tedious for a really long time."

"So maybe losing the job is a blessing in disguise?"

"I think so," he says. "If nothing else, because it's given us the chance to reconnect and be friends again." He pours more Frangelico into our shot glasses, and we drink. "Okay," he says, "your turn."

"Top five . . . let's see . . . um." It's been a while since I've played this game. "Top five . . . sandwiches."

"I don't think I've eaten any particularly memorable sandwiches recently," he says, "let alone five of them. Have you?"

I think about it. "No, I guess not. Sorry, that was a dumb one."

"Yeah, you're rusty at this."

"Fine, you do one."

"Okay," he says. "Top five most romantic nights."

"Like ever, with anyone?"

"Yeah."

"Um." This seems like a dangerous thing to be talking about with my ex-boyfriend. "I need a minute to think about it."

"Okay," he says, "I'll go first. The night we broke into the auditorium."

I'd worked as a costume assistant for one of the school plays, so I'd had the code to the school auditorium, and in the spring of freshman year we'd decided one night that we should go hook up there. I'd punched in the code on the side door, fingers trembling, half-expecting giant spotlights to come out of the sky and transfix us. But they hadn't, and kissing on the giant stage had been amazing, looking out at the rows of red velvet seats, all the way up to the stained glass windows at the top of the balcony.

"Yeah. That was fun."

"Cheers," he says, and we clink glasses and drink. "The night we went out in the canoe."

That had been junior year, in the fall. Ben's roommate Kyle had been into canoeing, and one night we'd borrowed his canoe and taken it down to the lake. We'd been apart all summer—Ben had been working as a camp counselor in Connecticut, and I'd been back home, folding clothes at a department store and counting the days until school started. That night we'd held hands, looking out at the dark water, and laughed at the simple wonder of being together again.

"The night of my twenty-third birthday," he continues. That had been when we were living together in the city. I'd spent over a thousand dollars to rent out the back room of Mangia e Beve, one of our favorite Italian restaurants. "Our first night in our own apartment together." We'd made love on a bare mattress, since we hadn't bought sheets yet. "And the night we first met and stayed up talking until the sun rose. Cheers." He raises his glass to mine again.

"Um. What about—what about Kelly?"

"Nope," he says. "All of mine were with you." He drinks, and to avoid meeting his eyes I drink too. "Even if you totally fall for someone later, there's something about first love, you know?"

I *do* know. I remember constantly wanting to talk to him, touch him, tell him everything I was thinking. I remember underlining passages in my books to read to him later. And when I wasn't talking *to* him, I was talking about him, almost incessantly. For a moment I feel more charitable towards Nat and Mel . . . it's really a wonder they didn't get sick of me back then.

And then suddenly I notice that Ben's hand is on top of mine, and our faces are very close, almost touching. He puts his other hand on the back of my head and draws my face towards his, and then somehow we're kissing. His lips are so familiar—I've kissed them so many times—that kissing him feels automatic, natural, like slipping into water.

We've been kissing for almost a minute when I suddenly realize I'm cheating on my boyfriend.

I pull away. "I can't."

He cups my face in his hands. "Look. Luce. I know you're seeing somebody."

"Yeah. I am. And I really—" I'm about to say that I really like him, but I'm overcome by a sudden wave of nausea from the knowledge of what I've done. I jump up and run down the hall into the bathroom.

I think I might need to throw up, but I don't, I just sit on the tile floor in front of the toilet for a couple of minutes. Once the nausea has passed, I get to my feet, splashing water on my face and staring at my reflection in the bathroom mirror. How did I let myself get into this situation? I've never cheated on anyone—never even *thought* about cheating on anyone—before.

When I come back into the living room, Ben is still sitting on the couch, looking concerned. "Are you okay?" he asks me.

"Yeah—I—I don't know what I'm doing—I—"

"Come sit down," he says. I hesitate, and he scoots over to the other end of the couch. "I'll sit over here. I won't try to kiss you again, or—or anything. Let's just talk."

"Okay." I sit down on the opposite end of the couch, leaning my head against the arm. Suddenly I want nothing more than to go to sleep. For about a million years.

"So I know you're seeing somebody," Ben says. "But I . . . I made a mistake."

"Yeah. This was a big mistake." I'm relieved that at least we're on the same page about that.

"Not this," he says. "I made a mistake when I let you go. I miss you."

Oh, God. I'm starting to feel nauseous again.

"I want you back," he says. "I realized it as soon as Kelly left me. You'd never have done something like that—broke up with me just because I lost my job. Would you?"

"No, but . . ."

He puts up a hand to stop me. "In fact," he continues with a sheepish smile, "I have a confession to make."

I'm not at all sure I want to hear this. "Yeah?"

"I didn't actually lose my apartment. I just said that because I knew you'd let me stay."

I sit bolt upright. "*What?*"

Ben actually has the nerve to look pleased with himself. "I did lose my job—that part was true—but I've got savings. I'll be able to pay my rent for another six months at least."

I think back to the single suitcase, the fact that he always had plenty of cash to pay for expensive dinners. I stand and cross the living room to the front door, which I hold open. "Get out," I tell him.

"What?"

"Leave. Go home. And don't ever come back again."

"But Luce, what about . . . I mean, we have to talk about this. About us."

"There is no this. There is no us."

"But we shared something tonight!" he says. He reaches out

to touch my arm and I shake him away angrily.

"We did not share something. You lied to me and took advantage of me, and now I'd like you to get out of my apartment."

"You don't—you wouldn't think about taking me back?"

"No!"

"Really?"

How cocky *is* he? "Are you going to put your suitcase outside in the hall, or should I?"

Ben hangs his head, goes into the living room, and begins packing his clothes into his suitcase. I watch him, without saying a word, until he zips it and drags it through the front door, and then I lock and bolt the door behind him, collapse onto the couch, and start to cry.

# – 25 –

I PRACTICALLY sleepwalk through Saturday. I go into work for a few hours and attempt to continue revising the press release, but all I can think about is what happened last night. When I find myself typing "tongue" instead of "toaster," I realize it's time to go home.

Saturday night my friend Candace from high school is having a party at a bar to celebrate her twenty-seventh birthday. Candace and I were close in high school because we shared a stand in the orchestra's first violin section, but she went to the University of Central Florida, and we didn't really keep in touch. We met for coffee once when she first moved to the city after college, and I invited her out with my friends a couple of times, but she was working as a paralegal at a law firm and quickly made her own set of friends there, and our contact since has been limited to the occasional Evite.

So I wasn't necessarily planning on going to her party . . . but come eight-thirty p.m., I'm desperately in need of distraction. I'm curled up on my bed trying to read *Sense and Sensibility*—one of the few classics we never actually got to in my Cornell English classes—and I've been on page forty-three for the past half hour. My progress isn't helped by the fact that I'm checking my phone every two minutes, terrified that it's going to ring and it's going to be Lewis. I haven't figured out what—if anything—I'm going to tell him.

So I get up and change out of my sweats and into dark jeans, boots, and a black tank top, and tie my hair back with Lewis' scarf. If nothing else, maybe being around people will provide a few hours of distraction.

Candace is holding court in the back room of Art Bar, in the Village, and as soon as I'm settled into one of their comfortable armchairs with a glass of wine I feel better. Some other girls I knew from the high school orchestra are there—Lisa Hannity and Joyce Kim and Mary Mulhaven, who all live in or around Manhattan now—and I haven't seen them in almost ten years, so there's the obligatory catching up on who's married (almost everyone who still lives back home), who's had plastic surgery (Katie Hanson—boob job), and who's dead (Chelsea Henley—car accident). And then Lisa asks me if I'm dating anybody, and I find myself telling them all about the situation with Ben and Lewis.

*Don't tell him.*

That's pretty much the consensus. "It didn't mean anything," Mary says, "so there's no reason he has to know about it."

"Plus, you were drunk, right?" says Lisa.

"And it was only a kiss," Joyce adds. "If Gary knew how many guys I'd kissed when we were first dating . . ."

And it's true. It certainly wasn't anything that would happen again. And it certainly didn't have any bearing on my feelings for Lewis. It was just a mistake, a stupid mistake . . . and after all, if Lewis had come home on Thursday or Friday like he said he was going to it never would have happened. There's really no reason he has to know.

I go home around midnight, after a round of hugs and promises to keep in touch and meet up again. I change back into my sweats, crawl into bed and sleep soundly . . . until six a.m., when I sit bolt upright in bed with a terrifying thought.

What if Lewis already knows?

He told me he can see it whenever somebody does something really bad. Kissing Ben wasn't *that* bad . . . not bad enough to get me sent to Hell (at least I hope not!) . . . but maybe it was bad enough that he would know about it.

I have to tell him.

And the thing is, even if he doesn't know . . . even if he has no idea . . . I still have to tell him. I can't build a relationship on a lie—even if it's a lie of omission. After all, then I'd be doing exactly what Lewis was doing when we were first dating, before I knew his secret.

I have to be honest.

I really don't want to be honest.

And just at that moment, as if the universe is reading my mind, my phone rings. Who could be calling me at six a.m.? I lean over and look at the name on the screen, and suddenly my heart starts beating fast and my hands start shaking. It's Lewis.

I think about letting it go to voicemail, but instead I take a deep breath, reach over, and pick up the phone. "Hello?"

"You're up," he says, sounding surprised. "I didn't think you would be. I just wanted to hear your voice on the message machine."

It certainly doesn't *sound* like he knows.

"I thought you were coming back Thursday or Friday," I tell him.

"I know," he says, "I'm sorry. I thought so too, it's just that everything ended up taking longer than I thought. So what are you doing awake?"

He definitely doesn't know. Which means I'm going to have to tell him. My heart sinks. "Um. Hanging out."

"Well, you want to come hang out over here?"

"Yeah. I'll see you in twenty minutes."

I put down the phone and get dressed in jeans and Lewis' cashmere hoodie, then go into the bathroom to brush my hair and put on some makeup. My hands are still shaking, and I try three times to draw a straight line with my eyeliner pencil before giving up and just brushing some copper shadow across my lids. As always, Lewis' diamond is nestled in the hollow of my throat.


AS SOON AS I knock on Lewis' door, he opens it and literally sweeps me into his arms, carrying me back towards the bedroom. "No! Stop!" I protest, but he ignores me and begins covering my face with kisses. He tosses me down on the bed. "Stop!" I say again, and he must hear something in my voice this time, because he does.

"Is something wrong?"

"I have something I need to tell you."

"So tell me."

"I don't want to tell you."

"Why not?"

I take a deep breath. "I kissed my ex-boyfriend."

Lewis pulls back as though I've physically struck him.

"Or, I mean, he kissed me."

"And what did you do . . . when he kissed you?" There's something dangerous in Lewis' voice, and I feel—as I've felt a few times before—almost afraid of him.

"I kissed him back. But then I stopped—as soon as I realized what I was doing."

Lewis stands, walks over to the window, and stares out at the city for a moment. There's something wounded in the set of his shoulders. The sky is just beginning to turn rose and gray with morning light.

He suddenly whirls around. "How could you not realize what you were doing?"

"I don't know. I had a couple of drinks, and I . . ." I realize how pathetic it sounds, and look down at the bed sheets. "There's no excuse. I made a mistake, a big mistake, and I'm really sorry."

"Well," Lewis says softly, almost contemplatively, "that doesn't do me much good, does it."

"It meant nothing," I tell him, "less than nothing, and I can promise you it would never happen again—"

He cuts me off with a swift chopping motion. "You should go home."

Hot tears spring into my eyes. "You want to just throw away everything we have, because of one mistake?"

"Of course, I don't want to," he says. "But I don't see that I have any choice."

"You could talk to me, you could try to understand!—"

"I don't want to understand," he says. "I thought you were better than that. It would break my heart to understand that you're not."

I'm crying openly now, tears streaming down my cheeks.

"But Lewis, I—I really care about you—"

"I was in love with you, Lucy!" he exclaims, and for the first time I hear the anguish in his voice. Then he reorganizes his features into a mask of control, and when he speaks again his voice is flat and cold. "Now are you going to pick up your purse and leave, or shall I pick it up and escort you?"

I bury my face in my hands for a minute, shoulders shaking, wanting nothing more than for Lewis to come over and put an arm around me and comfort me. But I know he won't. So I stand, wipe my eyes, go over to the corner and pick up my black tote, and begin walking down the hallway towards the door. Then I turn. I can't leave without asking this one last thing.

"You *were* in love with me? Past tense?"

"Past tense," Lewis confirms, and he walks by me down the hall to the front door and holds it open. I walk out, and the door slams shut with a final, definite thud behind me.

# – 26 –

I SIT ON the steps outside Lewis' building and cry for a few minutes, then stand up and start walking. I'm not walking towards the subway, or even uptown towards my apartment. I'm not really walking anywhere. The only destination that sounds remotely appealing is Lewis' bed, and I can't very well go back there. So I'm just walking.

It's seven-thirty a.m. on a Sunday, and the city that never sleeps appears to be sleeping. There are only a few people out on the mostly empty sidewalks, and almost all of the storefronts are covered over with metal grates. The sun is bright, but there's a chill in the air, and there are hardly any leaves left on the few trees planted along the sidewalk. Almost without my noticing, winter has started creeping in.

I walk past block after block of closed storefronts, empty restaurants and office buildings, until I end up in front of Century 21, the discount department store. For a moment I entertain a fantasy of going inside and buying something wildly expensive, a Gucci bag or a pair of Kate Spade sunglasses, to make myself feel better, but when I look at my watch it's only eight and the store doesn't open until eleven.

So I keep going, turning down streets at random until I find myself in the middle of a square in front of an enormous pillared church. A few people are ascending the steps, pulling open the giant wooden doors, and I find myself following them, opening the doors and stepping inside.

The interior of the church is vast and spacious, with rows of wooden pews, stained glass windows, and statues of saints in alcoves. People are seated in the first few pews, and a priest is mounting the stairs towards the altar. Clearly a service is about to begin. I hesitate in the back of the church, thinking about going up to the front and sitting down. I haven't been to a church service since before college, but maybe it would provide me some comfort.

Then again, church really doesn't seem like the appropriate place to seek solace for relationship problems . . . especially relationship problems with the *devil*. I give the assembled faithful a last look, then turn around and go back out the door into the sunshine. Back on the street, I see a subway station, and since I'm not sure where else to go, I go down the stairs and get on the E train towards home.

I get off at Penn Station and walk east towards my building. But when I'm standing in front of it, the thought of actually going inside seems unbearably depressing. There's a Starbucks on the corner, so I go in there instead, wait in line—there's always a line, even at eight-thirty on a Sunday—and buy a tall skim white chocolate mocha and a blueberry muffin. I'm waiting for my drink and looking around for a place to sit when I spot a familiar blonde head, bent over a laptop at a corner table. It's Melissa. Before I can decide whether to go over and say hi or look away and pretend I haven't seen her, she looks up.

Our eyes meet. She waves, tentatively, and I wave tentatively back. She motions me over, and I grab my mocha and carry it over to her table. "Hi," she says. "You're up early."

"So are you."

"Yeah," she says, "I haven't been sleeping very well." She gestures to the grande cup in front of her. "Thank God for coffee—I'm on cup number three."

"Three? How long have you been here?"

"Since they opened at six," she says. "What about you? What are you doing awake on a Sunday morning?"

I look down, break off a piece of my muffin and eat it while I think about what to say. It tastes dry and crumbly and has no appeal whatsoever. "It's a long story," I say finally.

"I've got time," Mel says.

"Do you? Because you didn't the other day." The words are out before I can stop them. I don't want to get in an argument, especially not here in the middle of Starbucks.

"I know," she says. "I've been feeling bad about that. You're my best friend, and I want to be there for you." She reaches across the table and puts her hand on top of mine. "I'm sorry."

I open my mouth to tell her it's okay . . . and burst into tears.

"Lucy? Lucy, what's wrong? Are you all right?"

I'm crying too hard to get any words out, and so Mel takes charge of the situation. She slides her laptop into her tote, puts one arm around my shoulders, grabs my mocha and her coffee in her other hand, and guides me out the door and down the street. I cry all the way through the lobby, up in the elevator, and for twenty minutes on the couch in the living room, until I finally stop crying long enough to tell her the story.

When I've finished, Mel sits for a moment, deep in thought, shaking her head. Then she looks up. "You know what this calls for?"

"What?"

"Emergency brunch."

Emergency brunch is a tradition that started our sophomore year at Cornell, when Mel was dumped by Jeremy Henley, the president of the junior class. Jeremy broke the news on a Tuesday night, and Wednesday morning, when Mel told us, Nat declared that we were all skipping our classes and going out for pancakes.

We had an emergency brunch when Nat sent a topless picture to her fling Sam Duncan and he shared it with his entire fraternity, and when Mel got rejected from Yale Law (she had to "settle" for Columbia), and we had them for a month of Sundays after Ben and I broke up. Somehow, there was nothing so bad that pancakes couldn't make it better. We haven't had one in a couple of years, though, and I'd almost forgotten about the tradition. But this seems like an excellent time to resurrect it.

"Let me just go in the bathroom and brush my hair," Mel says, "and then we'll go to Halo."

Halo is a local spot that features a prix fixe brunch with unlimited coffee, which both Mel and I could use. They're usually crowded, but it's early enough when Mel and I walk in that there's only one person, a tall dark-haired girl, standing by the doorway waiting to be seated. And then I stop short when I realize who it is.

Natalie.

She's facing away, and hasn't seen us. I grab Mel's arm and pull her back outside. "We have to leave. We have to go somewhere else."

"Why?"

"Nat's here. I really can't deal with her right now."

"I know she is," Mel says. "I called her."

"You *what?*"

"I called her before, when I went in the bathroom. She didn't want to come, but I told her she had to. She's your best friend, and it's time for you guys to make up." Mel grabs my arm and forcibly pulls me back inside the restaurant. "Come on."

# – 27 –

THE FIRST FEW minutes are excruciatingly awkward. I stare at
the tablecloth and rip my napkin into a pile of tiny shreds, while
Nat tosses her hair and makes eyes at all the men seated in the
vicinity of our table, and Mel attempts to bridge the gap and
engage us both in conversation.

"So, Lucy broke up with Lewis," Mel says.

"Lewis broke up with Lucy," I mutter.

"Good," Nat says airily. "He was no good for her anyhow."

"And Lucy's really sad about it," Mel continues.

"I don't know why," Nat says.

"And she really needs her friends right now."

"Well, maybe she should have thought of that before she
decided I wasn't her friend anymore," Nat says.

"I didn't decide!—" I burst out, and then I stop myself.
People at nearby tables are staring at us. "Look, Mel. I appreciate
the effort, but I really don't want to do this. I'm really . . . tired,
and . . . I don't know, upset, and I just want to go home and go
to bed." I push my chair back, get up, and begin threading my
way through the tables towards the door.

A hand on my shoulder stops me. I turn, expecting to see
Mel, but it's Nat. "Luce, I'm sorry," she says. "Come sit down.
Let's talk."

"I don't want to talk, I just want to go home."

"Don't go home," she says. I hesitate, looking back and
forth between Nat and the door. "I know I haven't been a
perfect friend, but I want to make it right. Please."

Reluctantly I follow her back to the table. "Okay," she says,
"here's the deal. The reason I got so mad about what you
said . . . is you were right. I really liked your brother, and it
freaked me out. A lot. So I went and kissed somebody else, and

now . . ." She looks down, then back up at us. "Now I can't stop thinking about him."

Mel and I lean forward eagerly. "Really?" I ask her. "Have you told him?"

She bites her lip. "No. I tried to call, but he didn't answer."

"I'll tell him!" I tell her. "I'll call him right now and tell him!"

"No!" she says. "Don't. I—"

"You what? You're scared?"

"Well, yeah," she says, "but that's not it. I want to tell him myself."

"How about I'll call him, and then you can tell him."

Mel raises her eyebrows. "Does anybody else feel like we're back in college?"

"College? I feel like we're back in seventh grade," Nat says. All of us laugh, and for that moment, I don't care where we are—I'm just glad everything is okay between us again.

"Let me call him right now," I tell her.

"Right now? I'm nervous!" She takes a big gulp of coffee.

"Too bad. I'm doing it before you change your mind."

"I'm not going to change my mind!" she protests.

"I'm kidding. I think." I take my cell phone out of my purse and scroll through the contacts until I find my brother's number.

"Hey, Luce." Jim's voice on the other end of the line sounds heavy.

"Hey. You sound tired. Did I wake you up?"

"No, just couldn't really sleep last night."

"Well. I, um—I have somebody here who wants to talk to you."

I hand the phone to Nat. "Hi," she says, biting her lip, and then quickly, "No, wait! I have something I have to tell you." She takes a deep breath. "Okay. I like you. I like you a lot. And I know I screwed up before, but it's just because I like you more than I've liked anybody . . . I don't know, maybe ever, and it scared me, and I'm hoping that maybe you'll give me another chance."

Mel and I watch with bated breath as Nat listens to

whatever Jim is saying on the other end of the phone. "I know," she says after a moment, and then "I know," again. And then, after a long pause, she smiles. "Okay," she says. "I can do that. Yeah. I'll call you tonight, and we can talk about the details."

She hangs up the phone, and announces, "I'm going to Kansas."

"You're *moving*?" Mel sounds horrified.

"No!" Nat exclaims. "God, no."

"Kansas is not that bad!" I protest, laughing.

"I'm sure it's lovely," Nat says, "but I'm just going for the weekend. He asked me to come out and visit. So I will, and we'll see how it goes."

"Yay!" Mel squeals, and I lean over to give Nat a hug.

"This is so exciting!" I tell her. "You guys would have the cutest babies!"

"Whoa!" Nat exclaims. "Let's not get ahead of ourselves."

"You mean you *don't* picture what kind of babies you'd have whenever you meet a guy you like?"

Nat looks at me in horror. "You *do*?"

Mel laughs. "I do too. I think it's normal."

"You and Lewis would have really cute babies," Nat admits. I sigh. "I know."

"Except," she says, "would they be, like, demons?"

"I don't know!" This hadn't occurred to me. "I don't want demon babies!" I sigh again, remembering the events of this morning. "Not that it matters now."

"Okay," she says, "so tell me what happened."

So I tell her the story. "I knew Ben was bad news!" she exclaims when I'm finished. "You're too sweet, that's your problem. You've got such a good heart that you figure that everybody else must have one too."

"Well," I shrug, "it was my fault, really. I screwed up, and now I have to pay the price."

"Okay," Nat says, "but you screwed up one time. I don't really think it was that big a deal."

"Lewis does."

"But honestly," Nat says, "if we're weighing 'kissed my

ex-boyfriend' against 'ruled over Hell for, I don't know, all eternity'? I think he ought to be a little more forgiving."

"That's true," Mel says. "You know I don't really subscribe to this whole Satan theory . . . but regardless, he's not exactly perfect."

"He's not perfect at all!" I exclaim. "I mean, he's great . . . but he lied to me and tried to get me sent to Hell when we first got together."

"Right!" Nat says. "And you forgave him. I'm not saying you should have . . . but you did. So I think he owes you the same thing."

"You're right! He does! He owes me another chance! But how am I going to get him to give it to me?"

"I don't know," Nat says. "Ask him?"

"But what if he doesn't want to?"

"Then he's not worth it anyhow," Mel says. The waitress sets down three plates of pancakes—banana walnut, chocolate chip, and strawberries and whipped cream. One of our emergency brunch traditions is that we each get a different kind, and then share all of them.

Mel serves herself from the plates, then looks up. "I have something to tell you guys," she says.

"Yeah?" Nat says.

She hesitates.

"Mel, what is it?" I ask her.

"Okay," she says, and takes a deep breath. "Brandon and I broke up."

So *that's* what's been going on. I knew there was something! "When? Why?"

"Actually," she says, "a while ago."

"What?" Nat exclaims. "And you didn't tell us?"

"I . . ." Suddenly Mel looks like she's about to cry. "I didn't know how. I always . . . have it together. I'm the one that has it together. And having it together doesn't include getting dumped by your fiancé because he found out you were making out with some stupid guy in some stupid club!"

And now she does start crying, which isn't a sight I've *ever* seen before, let alone in the middle of a public restaurant. Nat and I lean over and put our arms around her, telling her it's okay, and within about thirty seconds she's composed again.

"How did he find out?" Nat asks.

"One of his friends was at STK that night that you and I went there," Mel tells her. "Luce, you weren't there—you were out with Lewis. So Brandon's friend Jeff—I didn't see him, but I guess he saw me, and he told Brandon about this guy I was kissing. So Brandon got mad and confronted me about it, and I told him it was the first time, but . . ." She shrugs. "It wasn't, and he didn't believe me."

"So then he, what?" I ask her. "Just broke up with you right then?"

"Yeah. And then I tried to convince him to take me back. A few times, actually. But it turned out that some other people had seen me too . . . doing stuff, with other guys . . . and after they found out that he and I had broken up they told him. So. It's over. I'm single."

"Did you ever think that maybe . . ." I'm not sure if I should say this. "That maybe if you were making out with all these other guys, you didn't actually *want* to be with him?"

"I don't know," she says. "I always figured if I wanted to be with anyone it would be him. But maybe I don't want to be with anyone. Maybe I just want to be on my own for a while." She takes a sip of her coffee. "I've never been single, you know? I've had a boyfriend pretty much nonstop since I was thirteen. It always felt like one of the things I needed. Good grades, shiny hair, cute boyfriend. And Brandon was . . . I mean, he was perfect, he was everything I thought I wanted."

"Yeah, but that's not . . . that's not a good reason to be with someone."

"Then what's a good reason to be with someone?" she asks.

"Because you love him," I tell her.

"Do you love Lewis?"

I haven't said it—haven't even let myself think it—but as soon as she asks I know the answer. "Yeah. He isn't what I thought I wanted at all. I mean, obviously. But I do. I love him anyway."

"Then you have to go get him back," Nat says.

# – 28 –

WE ALL AGREE, however, that Operation Win Lewis Back will require some planning. So we decide to spend the afternoon engaging in another time-honored tradition that started in college: emergency shopping. Emergency shopping followed emergency brunch, and, given that the many of the stores in Ithaca skewed towards the eclectic, was responsible for such wardrobe treasures as Nat's lime green sequined leotard and my metal-spiked dog collar.

Today, Mel has declared that she needs "single clothes."

"Right," Nat says, "because your current wardrobe is so conservative." Mel has a penchant for showing off her marathon runner's legs in very short skirts.

"I mean, I have a lot of stuff that shows my legs . . . but I need clothes that show my boobs. Isn't that what single girls do?"

"I guess I need clothes that *don't* show my boobs, then," Nat says.

As for me, I need to find the perfect gift for Lewis—something that says both "I'm sorry" and "I'm amazing." Lewis has given me several beautiful gifts, and I've never given him anything, and it's definitely time for me to correct this imbalance. But what do you get the boy—or rather, evil demon—who has everything?

"What about a tie?" Nat suggests. "A really nice tie?" We've taken the subway downtown to Soho, and we're walking down Prince Street towards Intermix. The sun is high in the sky and it's turning out to be a beautiful afternoon.

"I don't know . . . he's not really the tie-wearing type."

"Or cuff links?" Mel says. "Does he wear cuff links?"

"Honestly, I have no idea." I have a very limited knowledge

of men's fashion.

"Or okay," she says, "What does he drink?"

And then I have it. "Scotch. Really nice scotch."

"Perfect," Mel says. "So we'll find a liquor store, and you'll get him a bottle."

A homeless man is slumped on the sidewalk in front of the coffee shop we're walking by. "Hey, beautiful ladies, spare any change?" he mutters. Nat and I shake our heads reflexively, but Mel stops.

"Actually," she says, "I do have something." She slides the sparkling three-carat diamond, which she's still wearing, off of her finger and holds it out to him. "It's from Cartier. You should be able to get a pretty good resale price."

The man stares at her, dumbfounded. She extends the ring again. "Take it. It's real."

Nat and I are staring at her, mouths open. Nat finds her voice first. "Uh, Mel? You really want to give him your engagement ring?"

"Why not?" Mel says. "I tried to give it back to Brandon, but he wouldn't take it. And it's not like I need the money. So I'll do a good deed."

Slowly, the man reaches his hand out for the ring. He turns it back and forth, staring at it in wonder as the princess-cut diamond catches the rays of the sun. It really is beautiful. "Are you—are you sure?" he says.

"Yeah," she says simply. He suddenly climbs to his feet and lurches toward her, wrapping her in a giant hug. Tiny Mel almost disappears inside his torn green army jacket, and Nat and I step forward in alarm before he releases her and we see that they're both smiling.

"Thank you," he says. "Thank you so much."

Mel inclines her head slightly, then quickly turns and keeps walking down the street. Nat and I hurry to catch up with her, and when we do, I see that she's blinking back tears.

"Are you okay?" I ask her.

"I'm fine," she says, quickly wiping them away. "Oh, look!" She points at a low-cut, wraparound, kelly-green dress hugging the plastic curves of a mannequin in the Intermix window. "That's cute, let's go in."

Forty-five minutes later, Mel has acquired the kelly-green dress and a low-cut silk shirt in three different colors: black, red, and hot pink. Nat, on the other hand, has acquired two surprisingly conservative button-down shirtdresses . . . and a pair of six-inch Lucite heels ("You can't expect me to change my style *completely!*")

And me? I normally don't even bother to try anything on at Intermix, since prices start around a hundred dollars and go up from there. But while Nat and Mel were flitting around the store, gathering armfuls of clothes to take into the dressing rooms, I spotted a deep red wraparound sweater hanging on the fifty-percent-off rack. I didn't even let myself look at the price tag, just picked it up and carried it into the dressing room, figuring at least it would give me something to do while Nat and Mel were trying things on.

And it was perfect. It hugged my curves, showed just a hint of cleavage, showed off my dark eyes and brought color into my cheeks. If I wore this, I didn't know how Lewis would be able to resist me. I checked the tag, and it was two hundred dollars—on sale from four hundred dollars, and still more expensive than almost anything I'd ever bought (for myself, at least . . . Lewis' gifts were on another level). But I had to have it.

So now we're walking back uptown, bags in hand, and looking for a liquor store. This being New York, we don't have to look far . . . within a couple of blocks we come across Soho Wines and Spirits on West Broadway. I'm not sure what brand of Scotch Lewis actually drinks . . . I've only seen him order it at bars . . . but fortunately the guy behind the counter is young, cute, and happy to help.

"Johnnie Walker Blue Label," he says, when I ask him what he'd recommend. He pulls down a bottle from the top shelf behind the counter. My eyes widen at the price tag: two hundred and fifty dollars. Suddenly I'm regretting buying the sweater.

Nat flutters her eyelashes at him. "Do you guys have any kind of loyal customer discount?"

"We do . . ." he says, "but you're not loyal customers . . . are you? I don't think I've ever seen you in here before."

"Well," Nat says, "not yet. But if you gave us a discount we would be."

He thinks about it. She smiles winningly at him. "Okay," he finally concedes, "how about this. I can give it to you for two hundred dollars."

I bite my lip and take out my credit card. I'll think about how to pay the bill next month. "Hey," the clerk says to Natalie, "would you want to maybe get a drink sometime?"

I shoot Nat a death glare, but as it turns out, I needn't worry. "I'm actually seeing someone," she says without missing a beat. "But thanks, that's really nice of you."

"Well," he says, "if it doesn't work out, you know where to find me." He ties a red ribbon around the bottle of Johnnie Walker, which comes in a blue box with embossed gold lettering, and hands it to me. "Gift for your special someone?" he asks.

"I hope so." The clerk looks confused. "I mean, it's for *a* special someone—but I don't know if he's mine."

"Good luck," he says. "I hope he's worth it."

# – 29 –

ONCE WE'RE BACK at the apartment, Nat and Mel help me get ready. I put on the wraparound sweater with my dark skinny jeans, and Nat lends me a pair of knee-high grey suede boots. Mel helps me brush my hair into a high ponytail and tie Lewis' scarf around it, and gives me a daytime version of smoky eyes. It's still more makeup than I usually wear for *night* time, but she and Nat assure me that it looks great.

I dawdle over choosing a lip gloss, and change my earrings three times before Nat and Mel tell me I'm stalling.

"Of course I'm stalling, I'm scared!" I exclaim. "What about silver hoops—don't you think those would look better?"

"Stick with the pearls," Mel says, "they're classy. And the raspberry lip gloss. And then get your butt out the door."

"Look," Nat says, "whatever happens, you're not going to end up any worse off than you are right now."

"Right now I'm just alone. If this doesn't work I'm going to end up alone *and* humiliated. And almost five hundred dollars poorer, between the sweater and the scotch."

"The sweater's gorgeous," Nat says, "and I'll drink the scotch. Now go." She picks up the bottle of Johnnie Walker, puts it in my purse, and puts my purse over my shoulder. Then she takes my right arm and Mel takes my left, and they begin escorting me toward the door.

"But what if?—"

"Good luck!" Nat exclaims, and closes the door behind me.

Heart beating fast, I walk down the hall and take the elevator down to the lobby. Maybe I should call first? But if I do—even if he answers—he'll tell me not to come. Better to just show up and see what happens. I walk to the corner and stick my arm out for a cab. When the cab pulls over and I climb in, I have the sudden impulse to tell the driver to go somewhere entirely different—like, say, the art museum! I haven't been to the Met in almost a year!—well, except for the benefit, and I didn't exactly get to see anything that night. But then I remember it's Sunday night and all the museums are closed. "Broadway and Rector Street," I tell him.

Fifteen minutes later, I'm standing in front of Lewis' building. I probably stand there for at least five minutes, just staring at the glass front doors, before I walk up the steps and pull one of them open. I recognize the doorman, an older, white-haired man with a round, friendly face who's often on duty nights. I give him a smile. "Hi—I'm—I'm here to see Lewis."

"Come to say goodbye? I'm sorry, miss—you just missed him."

"Oh. He went out?"

"He *moved* out," the doorman says.

I stop short in front of his desk. "He *what?*"

The doorman looks confused. "He didn't tell you?"

"No—we—we got in a fight."

"He had movers in and out all afternoon," the doorman says. "Put all his stuff in storage, then took off."

"He broke his lease?"

"I guess he must have. I wish I could tell you where he went, but I don't know."

And I suddenly realize that I do. "You said he just left?" I ask the doorman. He nods. I run out the door and back down the stairs, then stick my arm out for a cab.

"Canal Street RW station," I tell the driver.


AS SOON AS the cab pulls up in front of the subway station, I toss a twenty-dollar bill at the driver and jump out without bothering to wait for my change. I run down the stairs, fumbling frantically in my purse for my Metrocard, and managing to drop two tubes of lip gloss and my Duane Reade card before I find it. No time to pick them up . . . I swipe my card, run through the turnstile, and find myself on the RW platform.

I know if I don't catch up with Lewis right now, I'll never see him again. He'll come back to the city eventually, at least I assume he will ... but he'll live somewhere else ... he'll probably even *look* like someone else. I'll never be able to find him. Unless I do something terrible and get myself sent to Hell ... but I'm really not willing to wait until after I die to experience what it feels like to kiss him again.

And of course, it's possible that he isn't even headed for Hell. He could have gone to Vegas ... or anywhere else in the world. He could have shifted shape already. Or he could be traveling as an elemental, a fiery wind. But this is the only hope I've got.

And then, on the platform, I stop short ... realizing I have no idea which direction the doorway to Hell is in. I run to the left side of the platform and peer down the tunnel. Nothing but darkness. I run to the right side ... not that I expect to be able to see anything. Lewis had said the door was a ways down the tunnel. But on this side it feels decidedly warmer ... almost as though a gust of hot air is blowing from the tunnel up onto the platform. It's got to be this way.

I look the other way to make sure there isn't a train coming, then squat down, put one hand on the concrete to steady myself, and jump down into the subway tunnel. I hear a couple of alarmed shouts from passengers on the platform—"Miss?" "Hey, what are you doing?"—but I ignore them and begin running down the tunnel, staying as close to the wall as I can.

There's some light, but not much ... which is probably just as well, I realize when I hear a squeak and see a large rat scurrying into a hole in the wall in front of me. I keep going, half-running, half-stumbling, steadying myself against the wall, looking over my shoulder from time to time to make sure there isn't a train coming. The further down the tunnel I get, the hotter it seems to be getting, though there's no sign of a door in the wall yet.

And then, as I'm looking over my shoulder, I stumble over something and land hard on my hands and knees ... and the bottle of two-hundred-dollar scotch goes flying out of my purse and shatters in the dirt in front of me.

*Oh, no!* Well, no time to worry about it now. I grab the neck of the bottle and shove it back into my purse, with the vague idea that if I find Lewis, I'll be able to show him that at least I tried to get him something nice. I get to my feet, brushing dirt off my jeans—I've torn a hole in the knee, and it looks like I'm bleeding—and keep running, awkward in my high-heeled boots. I keep my eyes on the ground this time . . . I figure if there's a train coming from behind me, I'll hear it.

And then I do hear it . . . a low rumble that grows rapidly into a roar as a pair of white lights come barreling down the tunnel towards me. Suddenly I know how a squirrel must feel when a car is coming at it . . . I freeze, transfixed, absolutely terrified, as the roaring in my ears gets louder and louder. I try to flatten my body against the wall, desperately hoping that there's enough clearance for the train to go by me. And then, as the lights of the train flood the entire tunnel with stark white illumination, I realize that set into the wall, just a few feet in front of my outstretched fingertips, is a door.

I stumble forward, stretching my arm out in front of me, and push, and the door opens . . . and as the roar of the subway train becomes deafening, I throw myself through it, rolling on the ground as I land and the door swings shut behind me.

The first thing I realize is that I'm alive. The second is that my entire body hurts . . . my hands and knees from where I scraped them when I fell the first time, and now my back, elbows and shoulders, which bore the brunt of my landing. And the third thing I realize is that it's hot. Really hot. I can feel beads of sweat forming and beginning to roll down my face.

Gingerly, I climb to my feet. Miraculously, my purse is still on my arm, though it's slid down to my elbow . . . and its contents appear to still be inside it. I'm in a long tunnel, sloping gently downwards. The walls and floor are made of dirt, and lit by a faint red glow that seems to intensify as the tunnel curves downwards into the distance.

And there, in the distance, far in front of me . . . is it my imagination? . . . is the silhouette of a human figure.

"Lewis!" I scream. The figure gives no sign of having heard me, and I start to run again, stumbling awkwardly on the uneven dirt surface. I'm almost instantly drenched in sweat, and the further I get down into the tunnel, the hotter it seems to be getting. I can feel my hair sticking to the back of my neck.

"Lewis!" I scream again, and the figure seems to pause. I begin running faster. One of my suede high-heeled boots catches on something in the dirt and my ankle turns over. I gasp in pain . . . but it doesn't seem to be twisted, and after a minute the pain subsides and I can put weight on it again. "Lewis!" The figure is growing larger . . . at this point, it's definitely the silhouette of a man . . . dark suit . . . brown hair . . . it's him.

"*Lucy?*"

"Lewis, oh my God, I'm so glad I found you . . . I'm so glad I caught you . . ."

"Lucy, what the hell are you doing?"

This is not exactly the reaction I'd hoped for. "I came to find you," I tell him, trying to catch my breath. "To stop you from going. Or . . . at least to get you to tell me where you'd be when you came back."

He looks me up and down. "You look terrible."

I can only imagine . . . my carefully flatironed hair is falling out of its ponytail and sticking to my neck and my cheeks, I can feel my mascara dripping down my face, I'm covered with dirt, and I have a hole in my jeans. Lewis, of course, has somehow managed to make his way down a subway tunnel in his suit while looking immaculate.

"I know," I tell him. "Listen. You, um—" I'd imagined myself confidently listing all the reasons why he ought to forgive me. But of course, I'd imagined having the conversation in his bedroom, looking pretty and seductive, with a bottle of two-hundred-dollar scotch . . . not in a dark underground tunnel that leads to Hell. And now that he's actually standing in front of me, all of the reasons seem to have flown right out of my mind. All I can think about is how much I want to kiss him, how much I want him to hold me and look at me the way he used to.

"You . . ." I try again, and then trail off.

"Go home, Lucy," he tells me. "Go back to your ex-boyfriend—back to the world where you belong." And he turns and begins walking down the tunnel again.

And I'm suddenly furious. "You're Satan!" I scream after him. "You're the Lord of Hell!"

He turns around. "Yeah. So?"

"So I'd think you'd be able to be a little bit forgiving! . . . a little bit understanding when somebody else does something wrong! I mean, you expected me to get over the fact that you've spent centuries trying to get people to do horrible things and end up suffering eternal torment! . . . and I *did*, I cared about you enough that I got over it! And if I can get over *that*, then you ought to be able to get over the fact that I spent an unsatisfactory minute or two with my ex-boyfriend's tongue in my mouth! I'm not perfect! I'm not even good, not all the time, but nobody is! You of all people should know that!"

"I do know that—" he starts, but I cut him off.

"Okay, then start acting like it! You say you're ready to settle down and have a relationship, but you're never going to be able to have a relationship with me, or—or anyone unless you learn how to forgive people instead of judging them! I know it's your *job* to judge them, but it's a terrible way to live your *life*!"

"Lucy—" he says, but I cut him off.

"I made a mistake, and I told you I'm sorry . . . I ran down a tunnel and almost got hit by a train to tell you I'm sorry . . . and I bought you a bottle of two-hundred-dollar scotch to tell you I'm sorry—" I pull the jagged neck of the bottle out of my purse. "But I fell, and I broke it. So now you need to just accept the fact that I'm sorry and get over it! You told me once that I need to stand up for what I deserve, and I deserve for you to forgive me!"

We stand, staring at each other, for a moment. Then Lewis steps across the distance between us and takes hold of my shoulders. "It's not that you kissed someone else," he says. "I mean, it is . . . but it's more than that. It's that we live in different worlds—literally, and you don't . . . I mean, look at you, you obviously don't belong in mine."

"I was worried about that for a while," I tell him. "Maybe that's even the reason why I did what I did. But I'm not worried about it anymore."

"Why not?"

"Because I'd rather be here with you, in an underground tunnel on the way to Hell, than anywhere else in the world," I tell him. "I love you. And that means it doesn't matter what you do or what world you live in . . . I belong wherever you are."

Lewis looks at me, searching my face with his eyes for a long moment, then wraps his arms around me, crushing me so tightly I can't breathe, can't think, lose all consciousness of anything in the world besides him and his arms around me. He bends down to kiss me, a long, deep kiss that turns my knees weak and sets my lips on fire. He presses me up against the dirt wall of the tunnel and we kiss . . . and kiss . . . and kiss until I'm ready to tear off his clothes right there. Then he picks me up and carries me out of the tunnel and into the light.

# – 30 –

WE DON'T encounter any trains on the way back to the subway platform, though we do get a few puzzled looks as we climb up from the tracks. Lewis looks clean and polished, but I'm covered with dirt and scraped up, and the passengers waiting for the next train probably figure he was rescuing me from a suicide attempt. But nobody says anything . . . it's New York, after all, and I'm sure they've seen stranger things in the subway station. Besides, with Lewis holding my hand, I really don't care what anyone else thinks.

"Should we take a cab?" he says. "I think maybe we've spent enough time in the subway today."

I nod fervently. Lewis laughs, and hand in hand we climb the stairs and emerge into the fresh, chilly air of Canal Street. Lewis puts his jacket around my shoulders as we wait for a cab, but the warmth of his skin against mine is all I really need.

"So I guess we're going to your place," Lewis says. "Seeing as I don't have a place anymore."

"Oh, right! What are you going to do about that?"

"It was probably time to look for a new apartment anyhow," he says. "That last one was sort of . . . impersonal. Especially if I'm going to be spending most of my time in New York from now on." He smiles at me.

"Are you?"

"I hope so," he says.

"I hope so too," I tell him, leaning into the warmth of his arm and smiling up at him.

"What kind of scotch was it, by the way?" he asks me once a cab has pulled over and we're headed uptown.

"Johnnie Walker Blue Label."

"You broke a bottle of Johnnie Walker Blue?"

"I tripped over a rat!"

Lewis laughs and leans in to kiss me again. "I love you," he says.

We kiss for the rest of the cab ride, in the lobby, in the elevator, and then I catch a glimpse of myself in the mirror in my hallway and realize that before we kiss any more I desperately need to take a shower. "Oh, God. Do I smell as bad as I look?" I ask Lewis.

"You smell like roses," he says. "And subway exhaust."

I groan and unlock the door, planning to head straight for the bathroom . . . but Nat and Mel are sitting on the couch. When they see me, their eyes widen with concern . . . and then they look behind me and catch sight of Lewis, and start applauding. Lewis looks confused. "They knew . . . they told me to . . ." I try to explain.

"We're happy for you guys," Nat says.

"Oh," Lewis says, still looking perplexed. "Okay."

"What *happened* to you?" Mel asks me.

"It's a long story," I tell her. "And I've really got to take a shower."

"That's okay, we'll entertain Lewis," Nat says. "Sit down, sit down. Can we get you a glass of wine?"

"So Lucy tells us you're . . . the devil," I hear Mel saying pleasantly as I head down the hall with my towel. Oh, God. Well, I'll let them sort that one out on their own.

When I emerge from the shower, freshly towel-dried and clad in leggings and my Cornell sweatshirt, I find Lewis and Nat deeply engaged in a discussion of Nat's father, and Mel looking skeptical but listening to them politely. Apparently Lewis hasn't come across him in Hell, which is good. Nat's asking Lewis if there's any way to communicate with the dead, and he's telling her that there isn't . . . so far. Cell phones and email can't bridge the gap, and séances, unfortunately, have proven ineffective. Mel and I exchange relieved looks when Lewis says this . . . no more blasting AC/DC as Nat tries to break through the spirit barrier.

I cuddle up next to Lewis on the couch and take a sip from

his glass of wine. I couldn't be happier. Lewis and I are back together, my friends and I are getting along, my friends and Lewis are getting along . . . everything is right with the world, or at least my little corner of it. And then Lewis puts his arm around my shoulder and begins gently rubbing out the knots of tension there, and suddenly the heat of his fingers is all I can think about.

"So," Mel says, "we're going out! You guys want to come?"

I look from Mel to Nat. "You are?"

"I'm going to be good!" Nat says. "I'm Mel's wingman tonight. She's single now, so we're going to find her some boys to make out with!"

I refrain from saying that even when Mel *wasn't* single, she never had any trouble finding boys to make out with. "Thanks," I tell them, "but I think maybe we're going to stay in. It's kind of been a long day."

A few minutes later, hair smoothed and lipstick applied, Nat and Mel head out the door, leaving me alone on the couch with Lewis. "So," he says with a smile, reaching out to tuck a lock of hair behind my ear. "What do we do now?"

I lean in to kiss him, and, still kissing, we stumble across the room and into my closet. He kisses my neck and puts his warm hands under my sweatshirt, and I begin unbuttoning his shirt. He unbuckles his belt, takes off his pants, and I point at his black dress socks. "Those, too," I tell him.

"Really?" He begins pulling one of the socks down, then hesitates. "I don't have to. We can just—"

I reach down and pull off one of his socks, then the other, running my hands over the black hooves underneath them. They're hard and cool to the touch, like marble . . . and I notice, now that I look at them more closely, that they're not really solid black at all . . . a swirl of colors runs through them, like a rainbow in an oil slick on the pavement.

"They're beautiful," I say to Lewis in surprise.

"You're beautiful," he says in a husky voice, pulling me up to kiss him, and my skin begins to tingle all over as our bodies melt into each other, and I lose track of where mine ends and his begins.

Afterwards, I rest my head on his chest as he lights a cigarette with the tip of his finger, passes it over to me for a drag, then takes it back. And just then, from my purse, which I dropped in the corner of the room when I came in, I hear my cell phone ringing.

I climb out of bed, wrapping my white cotton robe around myself, and retrieve it, but by the time I get there it's already gone to voicemail. It was Jim . . . probably calling to gush about Natalie. I go back to the bed and lay down in the crook of Lewis' arm, smiling as I press 1 to receive my messages.

"Um, hi, Luce. It's me. I just talked to Nat. She's out at a bar, and she sounded kind of drunk. And she said . . . she said you were back together with your boyfriend. And then she said . . . um, she said your boyfriend was Satan. So . . . yeah. Call me back."

*Oh, no.*

I haven't even thought about how I'm going to break the news to my parents and my brother. Honestly, I was hoping I wouldn't have to, I could just keep putting them off with vague half-truths . . . but so much for that. As hard as it was for me to deal with the truth about Lewis, it's going to be that much harder for them.

I hang up the phone with a sigh, climbing out of bed to put it back in my purse again. "What's wrong?" Lewis asks.

I climb back into bed and snuggle close to him again. "Nothing," I tell him, wrapping my arms around him and leaning in to kiss his neck. "Nothing that we can't deal with tomorrow."

We're in love, and for right now that's all that matters. For right now, the two of us, wrapped in each other's arms, here in my tiny room, are all that matters. And everyone else will just have to find some way to accept it.Because I love Lewis, and Lewis loves me, and I have a feeling we're going to be in each other's lives for quite a while.

Which means that I'll be taking Satan home to meet my family.

# Acknowledgments

Thanks to my agent, Katharine Sands, for serving as such a strong advocate. Thanks also to Deborah Smith and Deb Dixon, and everyone at Bell Bridge Books, for believing in the book and for invaluable editorial and marketing assistance. Thanks to Lane Bishop for seeing the movie potential and optioning the book, and to Julie Sherman Wolfe for a great screenplay adaptation.

Thanks to Nick Romeo for reading and providing discerning commentary (on this and everything I write), and to Rick and Karen Romeo for reading and thinking it's wonderful, whether it actually is or not (re: this and everything I write). And thanks to Dan Ostrach for everything.

# About The Author

Lia Romeo is an award-winning comic writer. She graduated from Princeton University, then earned her MFA from Rutgers University's Mason Gross School of the Arts.

She is the author of the popular humor book *11,002 Things to Be Miserable About* (yes, it's just what it sounds like,) and of several plays, which have been produced around the U.S. and internationally. *Dating the Devil* is her first novel. She lives in Hoboken, NJ with her fiancé Dan and their dog, George Gordon, Lord Byron.

CPSIA information can be obtained at www.ICGtesting.com
Printed in the USA
BVOW03s1533041113

335436BV00004B/195/P